W9-BON-332

"You would make a good doctor's wife."

Deborah blushed. Dr. Wright was a nice young chap and Deborah had blushed twice at his name. Sir James wasn't sure why he felt a vague regret.

As for Deborah, the blush hadn't been for Dr. Wright; she had at that very moment made the discovery that if she were to be a doctor's wife she would want Sir James Marlow to be that doctor. Just for a moment nothing and nobody else mattered while she digested this exciting fact before she suppressed it sternly as a load of nonsense.

Betty Neels spent her childhood and youth in Devonshire before training as a nurse and midwife. She was an army nursing sister during the war, married a Dutchman and subsequently lived in Holland for fourteen years. She lives with her husband in Dorset, and has a daughter and grandson. Her hobbies are reading, animals, old buildings and writing. Betty started to write on retirement from nursing, incited by a lady in a library bemoaning the lack of romantic novels.

Books by Betty Neels

Don't miss any of our special offers. Write to us at the following address for information on our newest releases.

Harlequin Reader Service
U.S.: 3010 Walden Ave., P.O. Box 1325, Buffalo, NY 14269
Canadian: P.O. Box 609, Fort Erie, Ont. L2A 5X3

Waiting for Deborah
Betty Neels

Harlequin Books

TORONTO • NEW YORK • LONDON
AMSTERDAM • PARIS • SYDNEY • HAMBURG
STOCKHOLM • ATHENS • TOKYO • MILAN
MADRID • WARSAW • BUDAPEST • AUCKLAND

ISBN 0-373-03400-8

WAITING FOR DEBORAH

First North American Publication 1996.

Copyright © 1994 by Betty Neels.

This edition published by arrangement with Harlequin Books S.A.

® and TM are trademarks of the publisher. Trademarks indicated with
® are registered in the United States Patent and Trademark Office, the
Canadian Trade Marks Office and in other countries.

Printed in U.S.A.

CHAPTER ONE

THE man standing in front of the empty fireplace was short and stockily built with a long thin face and light brown hair already receding from his forehead. He was dressed in a pin-striped suit, a coloured shirt and a perfectly dreadful tie, and he was obviously pleased both with his appearance and his attire. When he spoke it was with a pomposity which was quite unsuited to his age and his appearance.

There were two other persons in the room, a young woman, elegantly dressed and faultlessly made up, her dark hair brushed into a carefully careless cloud around her good looks, who was lounging on a sofa, and another girl, considerably younger, sitting on a small chair by the window. Unlike her companion, she had carroty hair which was straight and pinned rather carelessly into a knot at the back of her neck. She had no looks to speak of and she was far too thin; only her eyes, when she glanced at the man, were beautiful: vividly blue, large and fringed with curling lashes several shades darker than her hair. She sat composedly, her hands clasped in the lap of her tweed skirt, and listened to the man as he talked.

'Of course I shall sell this place and the furniture. I may have to wait for my money but I have my flat and you, Barbara, have yours.'

'*I* haven't a flat,' observed the girl with the carroty hair in a matter-of-fact voice.

They both looked at her. 'My father was good enough to allow you to live here in comfort with him while he was alone, very generous of him considering that you are no relation . . .'

'My mother married him.'

Her stepbrother waved that away with a podgy hand. 'And since her death he gave you a home—a very comfortable home too—you have lived at your ease, Deborah, and I consider that I owe you nothing.'

'Yes, well—I thought you might think that.' She added in a small calm voice, 'You and Barbara have never liked me.'

'Well, you have no need to wallow in self-pity,' said Barbara nastily. 'You've had plenty of experience running a household, you get yourself a job—a mother's help or something. Anyway this is all very boring. Walter, I'll leave it all to you; just let me have my share when you've got rid of this place.' She got up gracefully and went to rearrange her hair in front of the old-fashioned mirror above the fireplace.

'Very well, it may take some time. I suppose Deborah can stay here and caretake until the house is sold.' He didn't ask her if she were willing but went on, 'I'll see that you have money for food and so on.'

He joined his sister on the way to the door. 'And don't think that you can throw my money around; I shall want accounts kept of every penny you spend.'

'There won't be any accounts,' said Deborah reasonably, 'because I have no money; you took the chequebooks as soon as my stepfather died and probably any cash there was in the house as well.'

Walter went an unbecoming puce and gobbled. 'Don't be impertinent, you know nothing about such things.' He took his wallet from a pocket and counted out some notes. 'You will need very little money; this should be sufficient for some weeks.'

He bustled Barbara out of the room and banged the door after him only to open it again. 'And kindly remember that this house and its contents are now mine.'

She sat quietly until she heard the bang of the front door—banging doors was Walter's way of expressing his annoyance. She got to her feet then, picked up the money and put it in her handbag and went along to the kitchen to make herself some lunch. She was alone in the house; there had been a cook and a housemaid when her stepfather had been alive but Walter had dismissed them with a month's wages the moment the funeral was over. Unnecessary mouths to feed, he had told Barbara; he wouldn't need to pay Deborah anything if she stayed at the house until he had sold it. She had nowhere to go, no family living near by, and her only friends were elderly ones of her mother. She had lost touch with them anyway, for his father had discouraged any social life which she might have had; her place, he had told her frequently, was at home, looking after him. It was, Walter had observed in a satisfied voice, a most satisfactory arrangement.

Deborah ate her lunch, got her outdoor things and left the house, walking briskly in the chill March wind. The bus stop was some minutes away, for her stepfather's house was in one of the secluded roads in Hampstead, but she enjoyed the short walk, her head full of plans. She was free; never mind what Walter had said, she would find a job as quickly as possible and leave the house. She could leave the keys with the house agent . . .

In Oxford Street, off the bus, she bought an evening paper and scanned its columns for agents' addresses. There was any number. She chose the nearest, stated her wish to work as a mother's help, paid her fee, and made her way to the second address she had marked on the newspaper. She visited four agencies and the fees made a considerable hole in Walter's money. Set a sprat to catch a mackerel, Deborah told herself, getting on the bus again to go back to Hampstead and the large unfriendly house she had called home for some years.

She had tea and supper together for it was already early evening, sitting in the kitchen, pencil and paper on the table beside her, doing optimistic sums. She had given her telephone number to the agencies; they would ring if there was anything suitable. In the meanwhile she would pack her clothes and—since it hadn't entered her head to do otherwise—clean and dust and Hoover the gloomy rooms until she was able to leave. She locked up presently and went upstairs to her room and got ready for bed. She didn't like being alone in the house but, since she had no choice, she tried to ignore the small noises and creaks which somehow only sounded at night. Tonight, however, she was too excited at the thought of her future to worry about that.

She didn't expect to hear anything the next day but by the end of the fourth day she was getting worried. A man from the house agent had been, inspected the house and told her that he would be in touch with her stepbrother, and it seemed to her highly likely that Walter would pay a visit in the very near future. She phoned the agencies the next morning and the first three had nothing for her but the fourth was more hopeful; if she would go along to the office perhaps she would like to consider a post which might suit her.

Deborah lost no time. The rush-hour was over, the bus made good time, and she found herself in Oxford Street, five minutes' walk from the side-street and the agency.

She was at its door when someone tapped her on the shoulder.

'Debby—it is Debby? My dear, such a long time since I saw you last—your stepfather died recently, did he not? Two weeks ago, wasn't it? Are you living with your stepbrother?'

The speaker was elderly, well dressed and still pretty and her smile was warm.

'Mrs Dexter, how lovely to see you—it's years...'

'So it is,' said her companion and reflected that Deborah's looks hadn't improved with the passing of time and surely she had been wearing that jacket and skirt when they had met last. 'You must have lunch with me and tell me your news, but first I must go and see that tiresome woman in the agency. You remember old Mrs Vernon? A friend of your dear mother's and of your grandmother's too. She had a stroke some months ago and now she is living with her niece who simply can't cope with her and has begged me to find someone to live in and look after her—a light post, she tells me, with a little housework and ironing and so forth. There's help in the house anyway but Clara—the niece, you know—tells me that she herself isn't too strong.'

Mrs Dexter drew breath and Deborah said quickly, 'Mrs Dexter, I need a job badly, as soon as possible—would I do?'

'You? My dear—but surely . . . did your stepfather not leave you provided for?' And when Deborah shook her head, 'And your stepbrother—I've forgotten his name—there must be plenty of money?'

'I believe there is, but Walter is settling things. He's selling the house—I'm staying there until it's sold and then I am to find work. Only I thought I wouldn't wait for that so I've got my name down at several agencies for mother's help or something similar. I'm used to running a house and looking after invalids.'

She spoke without bitterness and Mrs Dexter patted her arm. 'You have had more than your fair share of that, my dear. I believe that you would do very well for Mrs Vernon, especially as she has known you and your mother. We will go and see the woman inside and settle things.'

They mounted the stairs together and at the top Mrs Dexter said, 'I forgot to tell you, they live in the depths of the country—the Cotswolds, would you mind?'

'Mind? I shall love it, and Walter won't know where I am . . .'

Mrs Dexter paused on the landing. 'You had a stepsister too—a very pretty girl.'

'Barbara, yes, she has a boutique somewhere near Harrods.'

'She wouldn't like you to live with her?' ventured Mrs Dexter.

'She doesn't like me either,' said Deborah in a voice quite empty of self-pity.

Mrs Dexter said no more but swept into the agency office, dealt briskly with the stony-eyed woman behind the desk and swept out again, Deborah in tow. 'That's settled,' she said with satisfaction. 'I shall drive you down myself the day after tomorrow. Clara will be both relieved and delighted. Did I mention your salary? No?' She thought for a moment and mentioned a sum which Deborah, quite without money of her own for a long time, found unbelievably generous. They had coffee together in a chic little café and parted company the best of friends, Mrs Dexter to go into Liberty's and Deborah to scour BHS for the replenishment of her meagre wardrobe. Something suitable for the companion of a bedridden old lady and some decent undies—a dressing-gown too in case she had to get up in the night and sensible shoes, for presumably if her new job was in the country she would walk in her free time. Pleased with her purchases, she took herself back to Hampstead, and over her tea counted her remaining money. There wasn't a great deal left, but she wouldn't need any for the first week or so. Walter would be furious when he discovered that she had used his money in such a fashion but, after all, he had given it to her... She went to bed happy for the first time in years.

She spent the next day finishing her packing and making sure that the house was as clean and tidy as she could make it. She had thought a lot about writing a note to Walter and finally composed a stiff little letter telling him that she had found work for herself, left the keys with the house agent and turned off the water. He would be annoyed, of course, but it was unlikely that he would bother to look for her. She left the note on the hall table and went to bed for the last time in the house in the plainly furnished room her stepfather had considered good enough for her. Before she went to sleep she wondered what her room would be like in Mrs Vernon's house. Speculating happily about her future, she went to sleep.

She was to be fetched in the morning and Mrs Dexter's chauffeur-driven car drew up before the door shortly after nine o'clock. Sitting in the back with her mother's friend, Deborah was invited to ask any questions she wished.

'Mrs Vernon—is she Mrs Vernon's aunt?'

'No, no—Robert Vernon is her nephew. He and Clara have three children: two boys and a girl—let me see, they must be between ten and fourteen years old now, Robin, Ruth and Laurie. Clara has a busy life; Robert is a successful solicitor and has his office in the nearest town but they live near a small village four miles or so north of there. Eastleach—it's really two hamlets on either side of the road.'

'Is Mrs Vernon completely bedridden?'

'I believe so. From what Clara told me she remains in bed. The local nurse has been coming each day to attend to her but Clara has found it impossible to get her out of bed which is what the doctor recommends.' Mrs Dexter cast a rather worried look at Deborah. 'I hope that you will be strong enough, dear...'

'I nursed Mother for almost a year and when my stepfather became ill I nursed him too. He was a difficult patient,' added Deborah without rancour, remembering the disturbed nights, the constant complaining and the lack of freedom. She had tackled Walter once about getting someone to relieve her occasionally so that she might have a few hours to herself and had been lectured at length on the subject of her ingratitude. What did she expect? Had she not a cook and a housemaid to do everything for her?

Was she not fed and clothed? Had she not a comfortable roof over her head?

She had allowed his tirade to flow over her head and thought her own thoughts.

Since they travelled for a good part of the way on the M4, turning off at Swindon and going north to Lechlade, the journey took little more than two and a half hours. As they left the town behind them and took a narrow country road Deborah felt the first pangs of doubt. Supposing the old lady didn't like her? Or her niece for that matter? Well, she had burnt her boats now and there was no turning back. Her spirits lifted a little at Mrs Dexter's kind, 'You will be so welcome, my dear, and I am sure that you will be happy here.'

The car turned into a short drive and drew up before a lovely old Cotswold house, its walls and roof of honey-coloured Cotswold stone, its windows with stone mullions and leaded panes. Deborah got out of the car and looked around her with delight; there were daffodils massed in beds on either side of the house and clumps of them dotted around the well-kept lawns surrounding the house. It seemed like heaven after the house at Hampstead.

In answer to Mrs Dexter's tug on the bell-pull the door was opened by a stout little woman with a round smiling face and twinkling eyes, enveloped in a print overall. She wished them good day in a soft country voice and stood aside for them to go on ahead.

'It's Mrs Dexter and the young lady, isn't it?' She beamed at them both. 'Mrs Vernon's in the drawing-room—this way.'

The hall was pleasant and immaculate and so was the room into which they were shown, flowers everywhere, cushions well shaken, silver photo frames gleaming, and the woman crossing the room to greet them was as immaculate. Dressed in a well cut tweed skirt and a cashmere sweater and just the right amount of gold jewellery, she looked less than her years, her face skilfully made-up and her golden hair cut by a masterly hand. She was good-looking but she wore a discontented air as she kissed the air by Mrs Dexter's cheek.

'Aunt Phyllis, you have no idea how delighted I am to see you!' She glanced at Deborah. 'And this is Miss Everett?'

She smiled at Deborah but didn't shake hands and her blue eyes held no warmth. Deborah's heart sank. She doesn't like me, she reflected, and then decided that she had been mistaken when Mrs Vernon said, 'It is such a relief to me that I shall have help with my aunt. It is a light post and you will have plenty of time to yourself, but I lead a busy life with the children and various social commitments and I rely upon you to take good care of her at all times.' She smiled, though again the smile didn't reach her eyes. 'Do leave your things in the cloakroom and we will have lunch, then I can take you to my aunt.'

The dining-room was as pristine as the drawing-room and rather chilly. A grumpy-looking maid served lamb chops and vegetables and then jellied fruit and custard and Mrs Vernon and Mrs Dexter chatted lightly, careful to include Deborah in the conversation. They had their coffee at the table and presently Mrs Dexter said that she must go again. 'I must be back in town in good time,' she explained. 'I'm dining early, for I'm going to the theatre with friends.' She smiled kindly at Deborah. 'My dear, I'm sure that

you will be happy here—do write and tell me how you
are getting on, won't you? I am so glad that we met
at such a fortuitous time.'

Mrs Vernon went with her to the car and Deborah
sat where she was in the hall. Her case had been taken
upstairs; she supposed that she would be shown her
room and given time to unpack.

Mrs Vernon came back into the house, brisk and
businesslike. 'We will go to my aunt now,' she said.
'You can unpack later.'

Deborah followed her up the carpeted staircase,
along a corridor and then up another flight of stairs
at the back of the house. Here the thick carpeting had
given way to a serviceable matting and the windows
overlooking the country beyond were curtained in a
useful beige material. The passage they were in was
narrow and had several doors, the end one of which
Mrs Vernon opened.

'Well, here is your charge,' she told Deborah.

The room was large, low-ceilinged and sparsely
furnished. There was a long latticed window and
facing it a narrow bed, its occupant lying flat under
its blankets; an old lady, her eyes open, watching
them.

Mrs Vernon spoke rather loudly. 'Aunt Emma, here
is your companion. Her name is Deborah; she will
wash you and feed you and make your bed and make
sure that you are comfortable. I shall show her her
room now and then she will come back here to you.'

The old lady closed her eyes and Mrs Vernon said
impatiently, 'Of course, we aren't sure if she understands what we are saying. Now come and see
your room.'

It was separated from the old lady's by a bathroom, a small room, its narrow bed against a wall. There was a small table beneath the window, a chair by it and a basket chair by the bed beside a side-table with a lamp upon it. The bedspread was candlewick in the same serviceable shade of beige. A depressing little room, but Deborah reminded herself that it was hers, that she had a job and, if she saved her money, security for the foreseeable future.

'You can unpack later,' said Mrs Vernon carelessly. 'Go down to the kitchen at four o'clock and Cook will give you a tray. Aunt Emma has a drink then and you can have your tea at the same time.'

'Am I to have my meals here?' asked Deborah.

'She doesn't wake early; you can go down to the dining-room at half-past seven and have your breakfast then; I'll get Florrie—the housemaid—to keep an eye on Aunt Emma while you have your lunch and supper. You will have to arrange whatever free time you want but please don't expect me to relieve you. I'm completely worn out after weeks of looking after my aunt.'

'Is she to be left at all?'

'If she's sleeping there's no reason why you shouldn't get out for a time, I suppose; you'll discover when is best for yourself.'

Mrs Vernon went away and Deborah went back into the room. The old lady's eyes were still closed. She crossed to the window and pulled back the curtains and the pale sunshine lighted the room. 'A few flowers,' said Deborah, talking to herself, 'and surely Mrs Vernon would be more comfortable with another pillow.'

She went to the bed and studied the elderly face, one side drawn down a little by reason of the stroke. It must have been good-looking in earlier years and the untidy white hair curled prettily around it. Mrs Vernon opened her eyes, staring up at Deborah, who picked up one of the flaccid hands on the counterpane and held it gently.

'Hello,' she said in her pretty voice, 'I'm Deborah, come to look after you. I'll do my best to make you comfortable and I'm sure we'll get on well together. You niece wasn't sure if you understood her. If you understand me, will you wink?'

It was a nice surprise when the old lady winked. 'Oh, good,' said Deborah, 'that's an excellent start. I can ask you things and you can wink your answers. One wink for yes and two for no...'

It was a slow business but it worked. Within the next half-hour Deborah had turned her patient over on to her other side, peered into the other rooms along the passage until she found a soft pillow and settled the elderly head upon it and then, armed with a basin and water from the bathroom, freshened her face and hands.

The old eyes stared at her and Mrs Vernon's mouth made tiny movements although there was no sound.

Deborah pulled up a chair and took a hand in hers. 'Look, I don't know much about it, but I'm quite sure that you will be able to move and speak again, but you have to wait for your head to get better. I'll do all that I can to help you; we'll think up a routine for you and really work at it.'

She was heartened by the emphatic wink she had in answer.

She unpacked presently while the old lady dozed and then went down to the kitchen for the tray. She went down the way she had come up and as she reached the last tread of the staircase Mrs Vernon came out of the drawing-room with another woman, laughing and talking. She stopped when she saw Deborah and said sharply, 'You can use the back stairs, Deborah, but, since you're here, go through the baize door.' She nodded towards the back of the hall and went into the drawing-room with her companion.

The kitchen was large and comfortably warm and the cheerful soul who had admitted them said at once, 'You've come for your tray, love? I've got it ready, there's a feeder for Mrs Vernon and a jug of warm milk and a nice pot of tea for you and some sandwiches and cake. And if there is anything you need you just ask me or Cook. We're that glad you've come for we've been fair run off our feet since the old lady was took bad. We said to young Mrs Vernon, "You get someone to look after Mrs Vernon or we'll give in our notice".' She added sympathetically, 'You'll have your hands full, miss. Me and Cook'll take over for an hour in the afternoons so's you can get a breath of air.'

'You're very kind. I didn't know that you had had to look after Mrs Vernon; I thought young Mrs Vernon had been doing that.'

'Lor' love you, dearie, she never goes near the poor old thing, only when the doctor comes. She'd have been better off in an hospital but they want to keep her here so's if she gets to move a hand a bit she can sign her name so's they can take care of her money.'

She made the tea and put the teapot on the tray. 'Not that I should be gossiping with you, and you only just here but it's only right you should know which way the cat's jumping.'

'It's kind of you to tell me,' said Deborah. 'I'll take good care of the old lady.'

She bore the tray upstairs, gave Mrs Vernon the milk, a slow business but successfully achieved, and then sat down near the bed and had her own tea. Mrs Vernon was dozing again and she was able to consider what Mrs Dodd had told her—it was a quite different picture from that which Mrs Dexter had painted although she was sure that that lady had no idea of the true state of things. That her own position in the household wasn't quite as Mrs Dexter had pictured it didn't worry her; she was fired with the ambition to get the old lady better although she had very little idea of how to set about it. All she knew was that people recovered from strokes sooner or later and to a greater or lesser degree, provided that the stroke hadn't been a massive one. The local nurse had been coming in to see her and she might be a useful source of information... Deborah drained the teapot, ate everything on the tea tray and carried it back to the kitchen.

When she finally got into her bed that night she was tired. Mrs Vernon was hard work and she found that she was expected to manage by herself. It meant rolling the patient to and fro while she saw to the bed and washed her, heaved her up on to her pillows, fed her the milky drink which, it seemed, was all that she was allowed, and then sat quietly by the bed until she slept. The job, she reflected, wasn't quite what she had expected, but never mind that, it was a job and she was free...

She got up early and since the old lady was still asleep she bathed and dressed and crept down the back stairs. Mrs Dodd was in the kitchen and greeted her in a friendly fashion and offered a cup of tea.

'If you come down in half an hour your breakfast would be ready. You don't mind eating it here? The mistress has hers in bed and Mr Vernon likes to be on his own...'

Deborah didn't mind and said so and Mrs Dodd went on, 'You'll need to have the old lady spick and span by ten o'clock: the doctor comes twice a week— today and on Friday—just takes a look at her and has a chat with the mistress.'

Old Mrs Vernon was awake when Deborah went back upstairs and there was time to bathe her face and smooth her hair and make her comfortable. Deborah talked while she worked, heaved the old lady up the bed and turned her pillows and then offered her a drink. She drank thirstily and Deborah, of- fering more water, resolved to ask for something more interesting. Surely if Mrs Vernon could manage to swallow water she could do the same with orange juice or barley water or even Bovril and chicken broth?

Eating the breakfast the cook put before her pre- sently, she broached the subject. 'Well, I don't see why you shouldn't help yourself to anything you would think she might fancy. Fluids, the doctor said, and they're all fluids, aren't they?' She pointed to the big dresser which took up all one wall. 'You'll find everything that you want in there and no need to ask.'

So Deborah went back to the old lady's room with a jug of orange juice and a small tea tray. She hoped she was doing the right thing but she couldn't see any reason for not doing it and besides the doctor would come presently and she could ask him and find out too just how much movement the patient could tolerate.

The tea was taken with obvious pleasure, judging by the flurry of winks from the mask-like face. Deborah bore the tray back to the kitchen, put the orange juice in the bathroom to keep cool, and set about readying her patient for the day. Mrs Vernon, although helpless, was small and very thin, which was a good thing, for Deborah had a good deal of heaving and turning to do before she was satisfied with her efforts and knew that her patient was comfortable. It seemed that she was, for, when asked, she winked several times.

Dr Benson was a disappointment; he came into the room accompanied by young Mrs Vernon, accorded Deborah a nod and went to look at his patient.

'Looks comfortable enough,' he observed jovially. 'Let us hope that this young woman will look after her as well as you have done, my dear. I only hope that you have not overtaxed your strength; you must take things easy.'

Deborah, standing by the bed, saw the pent-up rage in the old eyes staring up at him. There was something wrong and she wasn't sure what it was but of one thing she was sure: it wouldn't be of any use asking Dr Benson's advice. He hadn't spoken to her at all, addressing all his remarks to Mrs Vernon, but she took heart when she heard him telling her that since she was so anxious about her aunt he had arranged for a specialist to come and see the old lady.

'I'll bring him with me on Friday,' he promised. 'He's one of the best men in the medical world.'

'You're doing very nicely.' He bent over his patient and spoke rather loudly. 'We must be patient.' He patted her hand, nodded to Deborah and went away with Mrs Vernon.

Deborah skipped to the bathroom and filled a feeder with some orange juice. Rest was all very well but some extra nourishment might do no harm. Her gentle heart was shaken to see tears oozing from under the old lady's eyelids. She put an arm round the elderly head and lifted it gently. 'You're going to get better,' she said, 'I'm quite sure of that. You're going to have nourishing drinks and I'm going to rub your legs and arms so that when you can move again you won't feel weak. I'm not a nurse but if you'll trust me I'll do my very best to get you better. Just don't lose heart, because it will take the two of us.'

Florrie came presently so that Deborah might go down to her lunch. It surprised her very much to discover that she was having it with young Mrs Vernon, but only for that day it seemed, so that that lady could make her wishes known to Deborah.

'Normally you may have your lunch in the morning-room at the back of the house and your supper too of course. Tea you can have upstairs and someone will sit with my aunt each afternoon for an hour or so. The village has a shop if you should need anything and when it can be arranged you may take a half-day—there's a bus once or twice a week into Lechlade.' She glanced at Deborah. 'It's an easy post—there's really nothing to do but keep my aunt comfortable. She needs very little and has no appetite.'

Deborah murmured politely, not believing a word of it.

She walked to the village and back while Mrs Dodd sat with Mrs Vernon. It was a brisk spring day and her spirits rose in the open air. It was nice to have an aim in life; it would be marvellous if she could get the old lady a little better—well enough to sit in a chair perhaps and eat a little and have visitors. Deborah went back to the unwelcoming room armed with a bunch of late snowdrops she had picked and, since there was no one to see, a few daffodils from the garden.

She showed them to her patient and thought that she saw pleasure in the staring eyes. She put them where they could be seen from the bed and went to fetch the tea tray.

The next day followed the pattern of the last with no sign of the old lady's niece and so did the day after that, but on Friday morning Deborah was surprised to see young Mrs Vernon come into the room.

'See that my aunt is in a clean nightgown,' she told Deborah after a meaningless 'Good morning'. 'Dr Benson will be here at half-past eleven with that specialist. Get the room tidied up too and remember to stand still and keep quiet while they're here; you have no need to answer any questions, for I will be here.'

She went away again, leaving Deborah to finish brushing the silvery hair and to tie it back out of the way. She smiled at the old lady as she did so and was taken aback by the look in her eyes. 'You can hear, can't you?' she asked gently, and when one eye winked, 'I'm going to try and see the doctor—this specialist who is coming to see you; I don't know how yet but I'll manage something—I'm sure there's more to be done than we're doing. Shall I do that?'

She had another wink in answer.

She heard Mrs Vernon's tinkling laugh before the door opened and they came in; she was talking vivaciously to Dr Benson and smiling charmingly at him and the man with him. He paused in the doorway and studied the room, its sparse furniture, the drab curtains, its lack of comfort; his eyes lingered for a moment on the bright splashes of colour afforded by the daffodils and snowdrops and last of all he looked at Deborah, neat as a new pin, her carroty hair severely pinned back, its colour vying with the flowers. He joined the others then and turned with a slight lift of his eyebrows to Mrs Vernon, then glancing at Deborah.

'Oh, this is my aunt's companion, or should I say attendant? She is quite a help to me—it is exhausting work, you know.'

The specialist crossed the room and held out a hand. 'But very worthwhile work,' he said and smiled down at her. 'Miss...?'

'Everett, Deborah Everett...'

Young Mrs Vernon broke in quickly, 'This is Sir James Marlow, Deborah.'

Deborah held out a hand and had it engulfed in his large cool one. He was a giant of a man, nearer forty than thirty, she thought, and handsome with it, his fair hair already silvered, his eyes a clear blue half hidden under heavy lids. She smiled—here was someone she could talk to...

CHAPTER TWO

DEBORAH quickly discovered that there was to be no chance of saying anything. Young Mrs Vernon had a smooth answer for Sir James's questions. Oh, yes, she assured him earnestly, her aunt had a varied liquid diet and she herself had massaged the flaccid arms and legs just as the nurse had told her to do. 'Quite exhausting,' she added, the very picture of patient effort.

Sir James had little to say; he nodded courteously and indicated that he would like to examine his patient. Deborah, waved away by Mrs Vernon's imperious hand, stepped back and watched while that lady turned back the bed covers, observing, 'Of course my aunt doesn't understand anything, does she? There is absolutely no response . . .'

Sir James didn't speak, but bent his vast bulk over the bed and began a leisurely examination of his patient. He was very thorough and when it was necessary to turn the patient from one side to the other it was Deborah who did it. 'For,' declared young Mrs Vernon, 'I simply haven't the strength.' Dr Benson patted her hand in a sympathetic manner but Sir James took no notice, intent as he was on noting reactions from his patient's feet. Not that there were any. Deborah replaced the bedclothes, squeezed one of the quiet hands on them and efficiently retired to her corner.

Sir James straightened his enormous back. He said clearly, looking at the old lady as he spoke, 'I see no reason why Mrs Vernon should not recover at least two-thirds of her normal capacity. Perhaps we might discuss what is to be done...'

'How splendid,' observed young Mrs Vernon, not meaning a word of it, and Dr Benson looked doubtful.

'It would mean treatment of some sort, presumably? But Mrs Vernon simply couldn't allow her aunt to go into hospital—here she has all the care she needs.'

'Perhaps if we talk about this downstairs?' suggested Sir James and smiled at Deborah as he left the room.

Deborah whisked herself over to the bed. 'He's on our side,' she said to the mask-like face on its pillows. 'He said that you would get better, you heard him, didn't you?' She received a wink, and went on, 'I must see him—if only he would stay for lunch I might see him when he leaves.'

Fate was, for once, being helpful. Cook told her that Sir James was staying to lunch although Dr Benson had had to go, 'Though he did say that he would have to be back in London later this afternoon. I'm to have lunch ready for one o'clock sharp so's he can leave by half-past two.'

Deborah, about to leave the kitchen with a jug of the delicious nourishing bouillon purloined from the dining-room lunch, paused to ask, 'Could Florrie come punctually, do you think? If she could come before two o'clock—I'll come back early to make up for it.'

'Don't you worry, miss,' said Cook, polishing the glasses at the table, 'I'll see she's there. Come down for your lunch as soon as you can. Old Mrs Vernon'll enjoy that bouillon—real tasty it is.'

Deborah talked while she fed the old lady, making plans about what they could do once Mrs Vernon was on her feet again. 'What you really need is a room on the ground floor so that I can put you in a wheel-chair and take you for walks. But first we have to get you out of bed...'

She went down to her own lunch presently and took her tray into the morning-room and closed the door carefully to shut out the sound of young Mrs Vernon's laugh. Deborah, a gentle soul by nature, really hated her. However, she had other things to think about; if Florrie was punctual she could be out of the house soon after two o'clock and since there was only one road to the village and the main road beyond it, Sir James would have to go that way. She would lie in wait for him, she decided, gobbling up the little dish of profiteroles Cook had saved from the dessert destined for the dining-room.

She had just finished settling Mrs Vernon for the afternoon when Florrie came and settled herself with a magazine near the bed.

'I'll be back by half-past three,' promised Deborah, and added, 'thank you, Florrie.'

'Meeting your boyfriend?' asked Florrie.

'With my plain face?' Deborah spoke matter-of-factly. 'I haven't got one—never had, not had the time nor the chance.'

'Well, I never, miss, and you're not all that plain, if you'd do your hair different like for a start—it's a lovely colour and I bet it curls a bit if only you'd give it a chance.'

'I'll think about it,' promised Deborah. She took a last look at the old lady and hurried off to get on her outdoor things; she had wasted time talking to Florrie.

It was the end of March and the month was going out like a lamb, true to the old adage. It was pleasant walking along the narrow country road but she didn't loiter; she wanted to be at least halfway to the village, well away from the house. If she remembered rightly there was a layby there; it would do nicely. All she had to do was to get him to stop.

She reached the spot and found it highly satisfactory for the road stretched on either side of it in a more or less straight line so that she would see him coming. It was merely a question of waiting.

She didn't have to wait long. The grey Bentley came rushing towards her in dignified silence and she stepped into the middle of the road and held up an arm. The great car stopped smoothly and Sir James opened the door.

'Do get in,' he said pleasantly. 'We can talk more easily.'

He waited while she got in and sat down and then leaned across her and closed the door.

'Did you know I'd be here?'

'I rather expected to see you...'

'Why?'

'You have an expressive face, Miss Everett.' He turned to look at her. 'What is worrying you?'

She studied his face before she replied; he wasn't only a very handsome man, he looked—she sought for a word—safe; besides, he was a doctor and one could say things to doctors and they listened and never told anyone...

'I haven't much time and I don't suppose you have either. I've only been here four days and I don't know anything about old Mrs Vernon. I was told that she was on a fluid diet and that she just needed to be kept comfortable but she had been having endless milk and water and—and she wasn't very clean. And somehow I couldn't get Dr Benson alone to ask him. I've started giving her some orange juice and Bovril and weak tea and she likes that—I know because she winks once if she thinks something is all right and twice if something is wrong. I turn her in bed as often as possible but couldn't I massage her arms and legs? You see, I'd like to help her to get better and not just lie there, but perhaps I shouldn't be doing any of these things. So would you tell me what to do and could you ask Dr Benson to write out a diet for her?' She heaved a gusty sigh. 'I sound like a prig, don't I? But I don't mean to be.'

He smiled very kindly. 'Not in the least like a prig, but why didn't you ask Dr Benson all this? He's a very kind man; it is hardly...'

'Oh, dear—it's something called medical ethics, isn't it? Silly of me not to think of that, but thank you for listening and I'll try to get him alone.' She put a hand on the door and he leaned across and took it off again and put it back in her lap.

'Not so fast. Leave it to me, will you? And in the meantime there is no reason why Mrs Vernon should not have variety in her fluid diet. No coffee, of course...you are familiar with the rudiments of nursing?'

'I nursed my mother for a year before she died and then my stepfather for more than two years.'

His voice was casual. 'You have no family?'

'Not really—a stepbrother and a stepsister.'

He nodded. 'There is no reason why Mrs Vernon should not improve considerably. By all means massage her legs and arms, and talk to her—you do already, do you not? Her hearing as far as I could judge is good.'

She heard the note of finality in his voice and put her hand on the door once more but before she could open it he had got out and come round the car to open it for her. She hadn't expected that and, much to her annoyance, blushed.

Sir James's firm mouth twitched but all he said was, 'Now do exactly as Dr Benson says, won't you? Goodbye, Miss Everett.'

She watched the car until it was out of sight before turning round and going back to the house. She was unlikely to see him again, she reflected, but she couldn't forget him; it wasn't just the magnificent size of him or his good looks—he had listened to her, something Walter hadn't done for years. Nor, for the matter, had her stepfather.

'A very nice man,' said Deborah, talking to herself since there was no one else to talk to. 'I should very much like to meet him again but of course I shan't.'

Florrie was deep in her magazine when Deborah got home. 'She's been as good as gold,' she told Deborah, 'sleeping like a baby.'

But when she went over to the bed the old lady's eyes were open. 'Good, have you been awake for a long time?'

An eye winked. 'Then we'll have tea early, shall we? I'll tell you about my walk...'

She described the primroses and violets she had found, the lambs she had seen in the fields bordering the road, the hedges and the catkins and a squirrel she had seen up a tree, but she didn't say a word about Sir James.

It was several days before Dr Benson came again and this time he wished her good morning. 'I have received a letter from Sir James,' he told her. 'I have already told Mrs Vernon of its contents but since you are looking after my patient it is necessary that I tell you too. He is of the opinion that the diet may be increased—broth, Bovril, weak tea, fruit juices—and he suggests that she might tolerate a nourishing milky food: Complan. You know of it?'

Deborah said that yes, she did, reflecting on the countless times she had prepared it for her stepfather.

'He also agrees with me that gentle massage would be of great benefit. Five minutes or so each day on the limbs.'

Young Mrs Vernon spoke, 'Of course none of this is going to cure her—but it might make her more comfortable, I suppose.' She peered down at her aunt, who lay with her eyes shut. 'She must be very weak by now.' She added quickly, 'Poor dear old thing.' Then gave Dr Benson a sad smile.

'You have done all—more than enough for her,' he told her. 'You are quite worn out—you need a few weeks' rest.' He glanced at Deborah. 'I should suppose that this young lady—Deborah?—is capable of taking over your duties as well as her own for a short period?'

Deborah, assuming her most capable expression, pondered the fact that Dr Benson, who was probably a nice man, clever enough and kind to his patients, should have been taken in so completely by Mrs Vernon. Probably Sir James felt the same way; she was by no means beautiful but she was skilfully made up and wore beautiful clothes; besides, she had mastered the art of being charming...

Dr Benson rambled on. 'You husband is still away? In London? What could be better? Allow yourself to relax, Mrs Vernon, enjoy yourself, go and join him, go out and about; you will return refreshed.'

Any woman, thought Deborah, listening to this, would be refreshed by a few theatres, dinners out and the kind of shopping Mrs Vernon would do. She wondered about Mr Vernon, apparently away on business. His wife spoke of him in capital letters so presumably he was her loving slave...

She caught the tail-end of what Mrs Vernon was saying. 'To leave my dear aunt with servants...I should never forgive myself if anything should happen while I was away.'

'My dear lady, your aunt may linger for some time; on the other hand she may die very shortly—she is very weak as you can see. Even with this diet which Sir James has suggested and massage...they are merely a means of bringing your aunt more comfort.'

'You think so?' Mrs Vernon sounded eager. 'Then perhaps I will go away for a week or so. But supposing she should die while I am away...?'

'My dear Mrs Vernon, no one is going to question your absolute devotion to your aunt and, in any case, she is unaware of anyone or anything.'

Deborah was standing where she could see her patient's face. She winked at it and had an answering wink. It was on the tip of her tongue to tell Dr Benson that his patient was listening to every word. She had her mouth open to utter when she received two winks and such a glare from the elderly eyes that she could only close her mouth again.

Dr Benson and Mrs Vernon went away presently and Deborah perched on the side of the bed so that the old lady could see her clearly.

'Nothing could be better,' she observed in her practical way. 'We shall have a week or more... I'll massage you and feed you up with chicken broth and beef tea and anything else that will go down. And don't take any notice of what they say. I know you are going to get better.' She added to clinch the matter, 'Sir James told me so.'

Mrs Vernon didn't go at once; she came every morning now to enquire as to her aunt's condition and Deborah told her each time that her patient had had a quiet night and was taking her feeds. What she didn't tell was that she had seen old Mrs Vernon's toes twitch when she had been washing her in bed. It was exciting and she was bursting to tell someone, preferably Sir James, but that wouldn't be possible; it would have to be Dr Benson and then only after she had made sure that she hadn't fancied it or given way to wishful thinking.

Young Mrs Vernon went at last, driven away in a taxi loaded with enough luggage for a month although she had told Deborah that she would return in a week, or ten days at the latest. She had also told Deborah not to force her aunt to take her feeds. 'We must allow the dear old thing to die peacefully,' she told Deborah. 'You are to let me know if you think that she is failing. Dr Benson will be away for a week or so, by the way, but really it is not necessary for the doctor to call. In an emergency you may telephone Dr Ferguson at Lechlade who understands the situation.' As an afterthought she added, 'You will be paid at the end of the month with the servants.'

A remark which Deborah found it unnecessary to reply to—just as well for rage at such rudeness was choking her.

For the first few days Mrs Vernon telephoned each evening. Then, since Deborah's report was always the same, she decided to telephone less often. 'Dr Benson will contact me immediately should I be needed,' she said and Deborah forbore from reminding her that Dr Benson was away...

It was four days after young Mrs Vernon had left that her aunt's fragile foot moved. Deborah watched it and tried not to get over-excited.

'Your foot—it's moving, can you feel it doing that? You can? Oh, Mrs Vernon, splendid. Look, I'm going to prop you up a little and then I'm going to let the doctor know. He'll tell me what to do. Dr Benson is still away but I can phone this other man—he'll want to see you.'

She went downstairs and shut herself in the drawing-room and phoned Dr Ferguson. Who wasn't there. 'He is on his rounds; no idea when he'll be back.' The voice was impatient.

'Has he a car phone? Will you try it please; it's urgent.'

'That's what they all say,' said the voice. 'Hang on.'

Deborah hung on, bursting with impatience until the voice told her that there wasn't an answer. 'He's not in his car, is he, then? Lord knows where he is. You're wasting your time. Try somewhere else or ring 999.'

Deborah replaced the receiver and stood thinking for a moment. Mrs Vernon had a desk in the sitting-room; perhaps there might be a telephone book on it, even a directory. Both were there amidst a litter of letters, bills and catalogues and right on the top was a small pad with a phone number scribbled on it and underneath the words 'Sir James Marlow'.

Deborah didn't wait; she made up her mind what to do and dialled the London number and almost at once an elderly voice said, 'Sir James Marlow's residence.'

'Can I speak to him, please? It's urgent—tell him it's about Mrs Vernon.' She added, 'Tell him it's Miss Everett.'

His quiet voice sounded in her ear. 'Miss Everett, how can I help?'

'Look,' said Deborah not bothering with the niceties of polite manners, 'Mrs Vernon's moving her foot— it began with a twitch but now it's actually moving and Dr Benson is away and the doctor I'm supposed to get if I need one is out on his rounds—they tried his car phone but of course he's not in his car. What shall I do?'

'Are you alone in the house?'

'No, no—I mean Mrs Dodd is here and so is Cook. Mrs Vernon—young Mrs Vernon—is in London and I don't know quite where, she said she would telephone. She's gone for a week or ten days so I expect she'll ring soon; she's been there four days.'

'Go back to your patient, Miss Everett. I will be with you in rather less than three hours. Don't get too excited.'

'Of course I'm excited,' snapped Deborah. 'Wouldn't you be if you could move your foot?'

A silly remark and rather rude and deserving of his quelling, 'Goodbye, Miss Everett.'

She had no time to bother about that now; she sped back to Mrs Vernon, pausing at the door to regain her calm before telling her that Sir James Marlow was coming to see her and since it would be lunchtime by then Mrs Vernon should have her chicken broth a little earlier. 'And I suppose I should warn Cook—do you think he'll want lunch?'

She received a wink and, obedient to it, went down to the kitchen and explained to Cook, although she didn't say why Sir James was coming; time enough for that when he had done.

'That'll be nice, Deborah,' said Cook. 'You'll have some company for once. I'll sit with Mrs Vernon so's there's no reason to hurry—you can have a chat with him.'

'He may prefer to lunch by himself,' said Deborah doubtfully. 'I'll ask him.'

She went back upstairs, armed with more flowers from the garden and, anxious to make a good impression, tied Mrs Vernon's hair back with a pink ribbon before brushing her own carroty locks.

Mrs Vernon, strengthened by the broth and nicely scented with lavender water, stared up at Sir James's face as he bent over her. He had arrived quietly, bade Deborah a civil good morning and gone at once to the bedside.

He took the old lady's hand in his and felt its faint movement. 'You're much better,' he told her, and received a flurry of winks in reply. 'I'm going to take a look at you if I may, since Dr Benson isn't here.'

He made an unhurried examination, spending a long time with the foot, testing its reflexes before doing the same with the other foot. Presently he said, 'Mrs Vernon, it is too early to be certain of anything but

I believe that you will regain a good deal of your normal movement, but you must go very slowly. Your hearing is excellent, is it not? Have you tried to speak?'

The old lady grunted.

'Splendid—your voice is there; it will return. Don't try and force it. Miss Everett...' he changed that to Deborah at the two urgent winks '...Deborah will continue to massage your arms and legs and you must drink everything which she offers you. If you were in hospital there is a good deal more which could be done for you, but your niece told me that you would be unhappy there so we must do the best we can here.'

He waited until Deborah arranged the bedclothes tidily. 'Is there somewhere we can talk?' he asked.

'Yes,' said Deborah, 'there's a fire in the dining-room—in case you would like to stay for lunch?'

She went over to the bed and told its occupant that they were going downstairs then and that Mrs Dodd would come up at once. 'I'll be up to settle you for your nap presently.'

She led the way downstairs, ushered him into the dining-room and went to the kitchen. 'If Mrs Dodd wouldn't mind going up for a little while? Sir James wants to give me some instructions.'

'What about his lunch?' asked Cook.

'I'll ask him and come and tell you...'

He was at a window looking out on to the garden beyond but he turned round as she went into the room. 'You were kind enough to invite me to lunch—perhaps we could talk at the same time?'

'Me too? You want me to have lunch with you? I usually have mine on a tray...'

'I very much hope that you will keep me company.'

'Yes, well, if you say so—I'll tell Cook.' She whisked herself back to the kitchen to tell her and then rejoined him.

'I'm so sorry but I don't know where Mrs Vernon keeps her sherry—and I'm not sure if she would want me to—what I mean is, I'm a servant...' She went pink under his amused look.

'I have to drive back to London presently...'

'Oh, then you won't mind drinking lemonade or something like that.'

Sir James, who hadn't drunk lemonade for very many years, agreed that that would be an excellent choice.

Cook, without young Mrs Vernon's sharp eye upon her, had conjured up a splendid meal: soup, chicken pie with a winter salad, and a steamed pudding, as light as a feather with jam sauce and cream. Deborah enjoyed every morsel, aware that young Mrs Vernon would have been highly indignant at the idea of her aunt's attendant sitting at the same table as Sir James and eating such an excellent meal.

Over the chicken pie she judged it the time to ask a few questions. 'Is Mrs Vernon going to get quite better again? And will it take a long time?'

'Not quite better, I'm afraid, but possibly able to walk with a Zimmer frame, sit in a chair, get around in a wheelchair and have the use of her hands. Probably the left hand will be weaker than the right. As to her speech, it may be indistinct and slow. I see no reason why she should not enjoy life once more, though. When is Mrs Vernon returning?'

'I don't know.'

'And Dr Benson?'

'I wasn't told precisely.' She took a breath, 'I'm sorry if I did the wrong thing phoning you, Sir James, but I didn't know what to do.'

He accepted a second helping of pie. 'You did the right thing, Miss Everett. I shall contact Dr Benson at the earliest opportunity and suggest further treatment. How long are you to remain here?'

'I've no idea. Someone I know is young Mrs Vernon's aunt, and Mrs Vernon was finding it hard work coping with her aunt—there was only the district nurse coming in each day.' She hesitated, 'I needed work and so I came here.'

'You have no plans at the moment? No intention of marrying?'

'No, none at all.' She gave him a questioning look.

'I do not ask out of idle curiosity,' he told her with a smile. 'I was anticipating Mrs Vernon's partial recovery and her need for a companion.'

'Oh, I see. But I think that if she got better Mrs Vernon might want to look after her again.'

'Perhaps. We shall see. You have no need to say anything to Mrs Vernon or Dr Benson. I will find the means of communicating with them at the first opportunity.'

They ate their pudding while he talked casually about this and that, interposing a gentle question here and there so that Deborah, off her guard and relaxed, told him a great deal more than she would have wished.

He left presently after another brief visit to the old lady and Deborah, her hand in his large reassuring grasp, wished that they could meet again.

'You must be daft, my girl,' she told herself, watching the car disappear down the drive. 'He'll not even remember my name in a month's time.'

Three days went by in which Mrs Vernon's twitchings and movements became most satisfactorily more frequent. Deborah, eager to tell someone about it, was delighted to see Dr Benson's car coming up the drive on the fourth morning. He entered the room with a jovial good morning and said, 'What's all this I hear from Sir James? He has asked me to go up to London and discuss things with him. Very surprising, I must say, and most gratifying.'

Who for? wondered Deborah under her breath and, at his request, gave a succinct account of Mrs Vernon's improvement.

'How delighted your niece will be.' He addressed himself to his patient, who stared back at him. 'It is most unfortunate that I do not know exactly where she is staying but Sir James has undertaken to find her. I only trust that she is sufficiently improved in health to come home and resume her special responsibilities.'

Neither of his companions had anything to say to this, Mrs Vernon because she wasn't capable of doing so, Deborah because she could think of no suitable reply. Instead she asked if she should rearrange the bedclothes so that he might examine his patient.

'Most satisfactory,' he remarked when he had finished. 'Of course we shall know more in a week or so and in the meantime I will go and see Sir James. He finds it a most interesting case.' He glanced at Deborah. 'And this is due largely to your care and sharp eyes, Deborah. Mrs Vernon will be delighted when she hears the news.'

She didn't contradict him but escorted him down to the drawing-room and gave him coffee while she wondered just how Sir James was going to find young Mrs Vernon; perhaps they moved in the same social circle, whatever that meant. She conjured up a picture of Sir James, magnificent in black tie and escorting some elegant beauty to dine at the Savoy or the Ritz and seeing Mrs Vernon, presumably with her husband, seated close by. What would be easier than passing on the good news? She was forced to abandon this colourful fantasy in order to give her full attention to Dr Benson who was reiterating what she must and must not do.

It was three days before young Mrs Vernon, accompanied by her husband, returned home. Deborah had just finished making Mrs Vernon comfortable for the morning when Mrs Dodd came to fetch her. 'I'm to stay,' she said breathlessly because she had hurried up the stairs. 'Mrs Vernon wants to see you. Got here not ten minutes ago. Cook's in a fine temper, I can tell you, not having been told and nothing much in the house.

She went over to the elderly lady and looked at her. 'Morning, Mrs Vernon, love. Getting better, are you?'

'I'll be back as soon as I can,' said Deborah and hurried down the back stairs and into the hall.

The drawing-room door was open and young Mrs Vernon was standing in the centre of the room. She turned round as Deborah went in, exclaiming peevishly, 'What's all this I hear? I saw Sir James in London; he tells me that my aunt is recovering from her stroke. I must say this is quite unexpected...'

'Mrs Vernon is moving quite a lot—she is unable to talk but she makes sounds and seems to enjoy her diet. She really is getting better.'

'What's this I hear about you telephoning Sir James? The very idea—you appear to have over-reached yourself.'

'Dr Benson was away and his deputy couldn't be reached; I thought it urgent enough to telephone Sir James who had seen Mrs Vernon and would tell me what to do.'

'There was absolutely no need for that. My aunt's improvement is probably a flash in the pan—all this excitement is so bad for me and just as I was be-ginning to relax. I shall have to speak to my husband. He agrees with me that this is all very upsetting for my aunt...' She turned sharply as Florrie opened the door. 'Sir James Marlow, ma'am,' and stood aside to let him pass.

He glanced from Mrs Vernon's angry face to Deborah's pallor. 'Mrs Vernon, I am on my way to Bristol and have taken the opportunity of calling to see you. I believe that Dr Benson is on his way here? We might perhaps take another look at your aunt together and discuss her future, for, most happily, I believe her to have one.'

He had shaken hands as he spoke and then turned to Deborah. 'Miss Everett behaved with great good sense in calling me; she is to be commended...'

He smiled at Deborah and added suavely, 'Your husband is here? We might have a talk presently.'

Mrs Vernon had pulled herself together. 'How very good of you to call, Sir James. We should be most grateful if you would take a look at my aunt.' She smiled at Deborah, her eyes like flint. 'And of course we are indebted to Deborah for her splendid care.'

Mr Vernon and Dr Benson came in together and Mrs Vernon said, 'You may go, Deborah. Send Mrs Dodd downstairs at once and tell her to bring the coffee.'

Deborah went without saying anything, her quiet face showing nothing of her feelings, only her eyes were quite startlingly blue; Sir James, opening the door for her, noticed that.

Later they all came upstairs and young Mrs Vernon fluttered around the bed, tugging the bedclothes and twitching the pillow under her aunt's head until Sir James asked her quietly if she would allow him to examine her aunt. Mr Vernon went away then and his wife stayed only long enough to watch the return of mobility in her aunt. One side, Sir James pointed out, had much stronger reflexes than the other but that was to be expected; only time would tell how great the improvement would be.

'Yes, well—perhaps you will join us downstairs when you are ready, Sir James.' She went away leaving the two doctors to nod and murmur and move their wise heads while Deborah moved quite quietly out of earshot. She would dearly have loved to know what they were saying.

Presently Sir James addressed himself to his patient. 'Dr Benson and I are of the opinion that a period of rest is all that is required for you, Mrs Vernon, preferably somewhere where you can sit out of doors whenever possible. You will need the services of the physiotherapist and someone to look after you but life must be quiet and without worry of any kind. Dr Benson and I are going downstairs now to discuss this with your niece and her husband so I will wish you goodbye. Dr Benson will inform you if I am needed again.'

He smiled at Deborah as he went and she watched his enormous back disappear out of the door with a feeling of despair. They would send the old lady to some kind of home and she would be out of a job but, more than that, she would never know if old Mrs Vernon fulfilled the doctor's hopes. Her niece didn't like her and would take the first opportunity to dismiss her. She composed her troubled face into serenity and went to sit by the old lady to gossip brightly about the future.

In the drawing-room Sir James, with guile, charm and an iron determination, was getting his own way. On their way downstairs Dr Benson had mentioned that the old lady owned a cottage: 'A charming place but rather far away on the estuary near Kingsbridge—secluded but near enough for the usual medical services.'

An ideal solution to the problem of Mrs Vernon's future, said Sir James blandly, a few months in peaceful surroundings and she stood a good chance of taking up some kind of life again. And in the meantime Mrs Vernon would be able to have the chance to recover from her weeks of nursing and anxiety. Her present attendant could continue with her since she was accustomed to her and arrangements could be made for the local doctor to attend her and for her to have physiotherapy.

Mrs Vernon opened her mouth to refuse, caught her husband's eye and closed it again. 'It could be arranged,' said Mr Vernon, middle-aged and anxious to have the tiresome affair settled. His aunt had money

of her own, a substantial fortune which he would inherit, and since it seemed likely that she wouldn't live
for many more years it would be very convenient to
have her out of the house. Her will was safely in the
hands of his solicitor and since she was unable to write
he saw no danger there. The girl Deborah might prove
a nuisance, coaxing money from the old lady, but he
could soon put a stop to that...

Sir James watched his face and guessed what he
was thinking. 'Of course, your aunt could remain
here; it would mean moving her to a downstairs room
so that later on she could be wheeled into the garden.'
A remark which served to make up Mrs Vernon's mind
for her.

'She shall go to the cottage,' she declared. 'It will
be a great nuisance arranging her removal but if it is
for my aunt's benefit then nothing is too much
trouble.'

Sir James's eyes gleamed beneath their lids but all
he said was, 'I shall be glad to consult with Dr Benson
when he considers Mrs Vernon fit to be moved.' He
then made his goodbyes gravely and drove himself
away. He had done what he could for Mrs Vernon
and for the carroty-haired girl; he had no doubt that
they would both be a great deal happier in the cottage
than they were shut away in that upstairs room.

CHAPTER THREE

A MONTH passed before Dr Benson judged it was time to consult Sir James again. Mrs Vernon was sitting propped up in bed now with quite a lot of movement in her arms and hands and dangling her legs over the side of the bed under Deborah's anxious eye. There had been talk of a physiotherapist coming twice a week, but it had come to nothing, so she had followed Dr Benson's instructions and massaged and rubbed and encouraged the old lady. Her speech was returning too, slurred and almost unintelligible, and each day she laboriously wrote little messages in a shaky hand, and all these little miracles were ignored by her niece, who visited her each morning, asked how she was and went away again.

Deborah, asking for a half-day so that she might go to Lechlade and do some necessary shopping, had been treated to a tirade concerning the pleasant life she led with almost nothing to do, her tiresome habit of asking for this and that that the old lady needed when everyone knew that they were quite unnecessary, but she stuck to her guns in her quiet way and got her afternoon off.

'You're nothing but a little prig,' snapped Mrs Vernon as she went to the door. 'Too good to be true—I wouldn't trust you further than my arm.'

Deborah did her best to forget the unkindness of that remark and took herself off on the local bus; she had her wages and since she had had almost no chance to spend any of them she planned to lay her money out on clothes more suitable to the time of year than the suit and elderly dresses she had brought with her.

Lechlade was a pleasant town; she wished that she had the time to explore it but the bus returned at five o'clock and she had only a couple of hours or so. She found a shop which suited her needs exactly. Hardly the height of fashion, but with a good selection of the kind of clothes she had in mind. She spent a long time there and came out on to the street laden and content. Two cotton dresses, a denim skirt, a couple of tops and a casual jacket, a meagre wardrobe but more than she had had for some time. She bought sandals too before having tea in a café and going back in the bus.

Back with old Mrs Vernon, she displayed her purchases—they didn't look much but the old lady mumbled her approval and Deborah regaled her with the details of her afternoon. 'When we are at the cottage and you have your wheelchair we'll go shopping together,' she promised.

She put on the skirt and one of the blouses the very next day since it was the end of April and pleasantly warm. She had to cover them with the plastic apron she wore when she gave Mrs Vernon her bed bath but it gave her a nice feeling, wearing something new. It was a pity she didn't have time to take the apron off as Dr Benson and Sir James came into the room. She hadn't expected them and no one had warned her. She was thankful that Mrs Vernon was ready for her day, her hair brushed and in a fresh nightie. She herself, she was only too aware, looked a fright in the ill-fitting pinny and with her hair coming loose from its bun and curling around her cheeks.

They wished her good morning and Sir James asked quietly, 'You did not know that we were coming?'

She shook her head. 'No, Mrs Vernon hasn't had her massage and she hasn't dangled her legs...'

'Excellent, for now we can see her progress for ourselves.' Sir James flashed her a friendly smile. 'I have an excellent report from Dr Benson.'

The doctor's examination was lengthy and very thorough. Finally, Sir James straightened himself to his full height. 'I am of the opinion that Mrs Vernon is fit enough to travel to the cottage in Devon. All arrangements must be made, of course, so that she is conveyed there with the least possible stress to herself. The local doctor must be informed and the cottage must be made ready for her.' He glanced at Deborah, standing quietly by the bed. 'It would be ideal if Miss Everett were to go there first and make sure that everything was ready to receive Mrs Vernon...'

'I'm sure that could be arranged. We might discuss it with Mrs Vernon when we go downstairs. She will be only too glad to arrange whatever is necessary for the well-being of her aunt.'

Deborah kept her eyes on the bed, the carroty lashes sweeping her cheeks. Mrs Vernon junior wouldn't be glad at all but it looked as though Sir James would persuade her.

Which he did, for she came upstairs later that day in order to tell Deborah and her aunt what had been arranged. Deborah was to travel down by rail and open up the cottage, fetch provisions, see that the gas and electricity had been turned on, put the place in order and be ready to receive the old lady when she arrived. 'You will have to make your own way there,' said Mrs Vernon. 'Train, I suppose although I believe you won't get further than Totnes—there will be buses—you can find out when you get there.'

Not very satisfactory, reflected Deborah; on the other hand once they were there it would be worth all the hassle.

'You will be given your fare,' said Mrs Vernon as she left the room. 'I'll let you know when you are to go—two days before the ambulance should give you ample time to get the place ready.'

It was another three days before Deborah was told that she was to leave on the following day. 'Heaven knows how I am to manage,' complained young Mrs Vernon. 'I have arranged for the district nurse to come, of course; I am not strong enough to look after my aunt, as you well know. Pack whatever you think she may need and leave it ready; you can take your suitcase with you.'

All of which Deborah passed on to her patient before setting to and packing for the old lady. She had already prudently sorted out what she thought might be needed.

She didn't like leaving old Mrs Vernon and she dreaded the journey before her—bus to Swindon, train to Bristol where she would have to change, and go on to Exeter, where she would change yet again for Totnes and from there hopefully there would be a bus.

She set off early in the morning with a packet of sandwiches from Cook, an apple from Mrs Dodd and the memory of old Mrs Vernon's unhappy face very vivid in her mind. Young Mrs Vernon had given her money for her fare and sufficient to buy a supply of food for the cottage with the injunction that she was to keep a strict account of what she spent. 'This whole thing is nonsense,' she declared. 'Much better to have left my aunt in peace; this upheaval will kill her.'

To which Deborah made no reply.

The bus took a long time to get to Swindon but it stopped outside the station so that she caught her train. It would take less than an hour to get to Bristol and when there she would have ample time to get the Exeter train. Dr Benson, to her surprise, had written out the times of the trains for her and the journey, although long, had been well planned. She got off the train at Bristol and crossed over the platform to where the train to Exeter would leave. Her case was heavy and she would have liked a cup of coffee but there wasn't much time before the train left and the platform was crowded. She put the case down and looked around her for a porter or someone who could tell her this was indeed the right train, but there wasn't one in sight. She put down her hand to pick up her case once more, but it wasn't there; Sir James Marlow, standing just behind her, had it.

'I was afraid I would miss you,' he told her casually. 'The car's outside; come along.'

'Where to?' She was so pleased to see him that she felt quite giddy with gladness but she wasn't going to be hustled into something she knew nothing about. Being a polite girl, she added, 'Good morning, Sir James.'

'Dr Benson mentioned that you would be on this train and I am on my way to Plymouth. It seemed worth coming along to see if you were here.'

'I'm not going to Plymouth,' said Deborah.

'Don't split hairs, Deborah—I may call you Deborah? I have to pass within a few miles of South

Pool and it is not any trouble to drop you off on my way.'

He had a hand under her elbow, urging her gently but firmly the way she had come and then out of the station. 'Such a tedious journey by train if you are not able to catch the direct one,' he observed placidly, 'and I should imagine you might have difficulty in finding a bus from Totnes.'

He opened the car door as he spoke and shoved her gently inside, put her case in the boot and got in beside her. 'It will be pleasant to have someone to talk to,' he told her. 'Do you know Devon at all?'

'Torquay—we used to go there when I was a little girl. You're sure you don't mind? It may make you late in Plymouth.'

'No, no, I have a consultation there in the morning; I'm not in any hurry today...'

It took time to get out of Bristol and on to the motorway but once on that he drove steadily, not saying much, until they reached a service station. 'Coffee?' he asked her and when she nodded ushered her into a restaurant, found her a table and ordered coffee. They had to wait some time for it and he talked idly about nothing much, studying her as he did so. She had no looks to speak of, he reflected, although she had beautiful eyes and a lovely clear skin. Her hair was eye-catching, certainly, but she wore it bundled into a bun, which, although neat, did nothing to enhance her looks. He wondered why he had gone to some inconvenience to drive her to South Pool; he supposed it was pity, for she wasn't getting much fun out of life and she had gone to a great deal of trouble for old Mrs Vernon—and yet she wouldn't thank him for pitying her. Under that quiet exterior he sensed that there was a determined young woman lurking. If she were to discover that Dr Benson, at his request, had given him the particulars of her journey she would probably get up and walk away and thumb a lift for the rest of the journey rather than stay with him. He couldn't for the life of him think what had possessed him to arrange to drive her there other than pity and then concluded that he didn't pity her after all. He was sorry for her and he admired the way she kept cool under Mrs Vernon's evident dislike. He was a kind man and he sensed that she wasn't happy. Other girls might have walked out on Mrs Vernon weeks ago and found themselves a better job, but she wasn't other girls . . .

He shrugged the thought away as the coffee arrived and began an easy flow of talk calculated to put her at her ease.

Presently he drove on, talking casually from time to time, and Deborah began to enjoy herself. The big car was comfortable, devouring the road with silent ease, and her companion's imperturbable manner was soothing. She reflected wryly that she hadn't been like a normal person for a long time—Walter and Barbara had made sure of that and young Mrs Vernon had continued in the same manner. She found herself wishing that she had done her face and hair more carefully and worn something other than the denim skirt and cotton top, and, more than that, hadn't spent several years looking after a cold-hearted stepfather and thus missed the opportunity of meeting people of her own age. Not that Sir James was her age; she had already decided that he must be nearer forty than thirty, certainly married and with children.

'Do you live in London?' she asked him.

'Yes—it's convenient for the hospitals, but I do have a small place in the country.'

She wanted to ask where that might be but something in his placid voice stopped her; instead she remarked about the charm of the countryside they were passing through and then lapsed into silence. She had plenty to think about; there were provisions to get in, beds to make up, the cottage to air and warm and make welcome ...

'We will stop for lunch,' she was told by Sir James. 'Buckfastleigh is just ahead of us; we turn off there and, if I remember rightly, there is a pub close by.'

It was more of a road house than a pub, nicely furnished and warm and surprisingly well filled with customers. Deborah chose soup and a roll and a cup of coffee; she was hungry enough to eat more than that but she supposed that her companion wouldn't want to waste time sitting over a meal. They were on their way again in less than half an hour; a country road with high hedges and a great many corners and Sir James, with no sign of impatience, slowed his pace.

'Totnes next,' he told her, 'and then Kingsbridge—we shall be there in an hour.'

It was rather less than that as he went through Kingsbridge, following the river out of the town and then turning off to take a country road along its further bank, the road narrowing close to the water's edge and hemmed in by trees and undergrowth. Deborah wondered uneasily what would happen if they were to meet another car; the Bentley was already taking up more than its share of the road. They met nothing, although they passed a number of houses, well away from the road, among the trees. They were of a comfortable size and all of them had at least one garage.

The road left the river, going uphill and then levelling out into the village street, lined with houses and old cottages and with a large church looming beyond them.

'The first turning on the left; it's a cul-de-sac. The end cottage—called Frog Cottage.'

Sir James slowed the Bentley and eased the car through the narrow opening which widened into a quite wide expanse of grass, ringed by charming cottages, leaning against each other, and all different. Several of them had their doors open and a variety of faces looked out at them as he stopped before the last cottage along one side. It was larger than its neighbours, pink-washed and thatched with small latticed windows.

'I have to fetch the key from the neighbour,' said Deborah, and prepared to get out, to be stopped by Sir James.

'I'll fetch it—wait here.'

He came back presently after a brief conversation with a cosily plump woman, the key in his hand. He opened the car door, offered Deborah the key and stood beside her while she unlocked the door. The key was large and heavy and he took it from her and hung it on a nail just inside the door, put there, it seemed, for that very purpose.

The door opened into the sitting-room, quite a large, low-ceilinged room, rather dark but nicely furnished with small old-fashioned chairs, a sofa and a round table under the window. There was a door at the back of the room with an old-fashioned latch and beyond a small narrow kitchen well equipped and in turn leading to a glassed-in sun-room with a door into the small garden. The stairs were behind another door in the kitchen and Deborah said worriedly, 'But Mrs Vernon must stay down here...'

Sir James had gone back into the sitting-room and opened yet another door opposite the fireplace. It was smaller than the sitting-room but nicely furnished as a bedroom. 'Ideal,' he observed. 'As soon as the local doctor calls, get him to borrow a wheelchair—the door's wide enough. Mrs Vernon won't need to stay all day in her room and if it is fine weather she can sit outside. Let us go upstairs.'

There were two rooms upstairs, both small but here again nicely furnished and between them there was a very small bathroom. They stood on the tiny landing between the rooms and looked around then. 'Quite agreeable and very adequate,' said Sir James, and Deborah agreed. They were distinctly overcrowded in the small space but just with Mrs Vernon and herself there would be ample room. They went downstairs again and she opened a window—the cottage was clean even if dusty, but it needed a good airing. She would see to that as soon as Sir James had gone...

'It seems rather late for tea,' he remarked, leaning against the kitchen door, 'but I imagine the pub's open—it's just turned five o'clock. We'll go and have a meal before you start your housework.'

'But you'll be so late,' began Deborah.

'Plymouth is no distance; besides, I'm hungry.'

The pub was simply a stone's throw away, tucked neatly into the side of the village street with a small courtyard leading to its door. Sir James paused before they entered. 'Have you food with you? Tea, coffee...?'

'No, I thought I'd get it in the morning.'

He glanced across the street to a shop, Post Office and greengrocer's all rolled into one. 'Let us shop first. Were you given money by Mrs Vernon?'

'Oh, yes, and I'm to be sent money each week, enough for us both...'

'How much?'

She told him and he raised his brows although he said nothing. 'You have a list?'

She took it from her pocket and he glanced at its length. 'Well, if you were to buy sufficient for your breakfast. Say we do that?'

The shopkeeper was helpful; milk, bread, tea and sugar, butter and eggs were produced without haste while Deborah was questioned about her arrival. Of course everyone knew old Mrs Vernon, she hadn't been back for several years but she wasn't forgotten. It would be nice to see her again. 'You're looking after her, love? And your husband here?'

'He's not my husband,' said Deborah, very pink in the face, not daring to look at Sir James, sitting comfortably on a sack of potatoes and taking no part in the conversation.

She paid presently and he took the plastic bag from her and walked her back to the pub. It was small inside, with tables dotted around, a bar and a cheerful little fire burning in the old-fashioned grate.

Tea was no problem, they were told, and how about something to eat?

The tea came and with it a dish of pasties and a salad. The pasties were delicious and they emptied the dish between them and if Sir James, drinking his second cup of strong tea, found the meal rather different from his usual fare, he didn't say so. They didn't actually talk much and all the while Deborah was conscious that this was the last time she would see him. It was unlikely that he would be called in for a consultation again; Mrs Vernon was doing well and Dr Benson would look after her.

Presently they went back to the cottage and Sir James got into his car after wishing her a casual goodbye, dismissing her little speech of thanks with easy good manners.

She watched the Bentley turn into the street and went back into the cottage, tidied away the food, and then went from room to room, making sure that she knew where everything was. The place was well equipped, there was a telephone, a minute electric cooker and electric fires in the bedrooms. The sitting-room had an open fire and when she searched outside the sun-room she found kindling and coal. A fire would be cosy and welcoming for Mrs Vernon when she arrived. She opened windows, turned on the water and poked around the linen cupboard on the tiny landing; there were sheets and pillowcases and blankets in abundance and a couple of eiderdowns. She made up a bed in one of the upstairs bedrooms, unpacked her case and went downstairs again to make a pot of tea before she went to bed. It had been a long day—a long one for Sir James too; she hoped that he had arrived safely at wherever he was going. Was he going to a hospital there, she wondered, or to stay with friends? A waste of time thinking about him, she told herself, and went to bed.

There was very little time to think about him during the next day; she did spare a few moments while she was Hoovering and dusting and getting the little place ready, but being a practical girl she didn't allow them to deter her thoughts from practical ones and as soon as she had everything just so she took the shopping basket from behind the kitchen door and went across to the village stores, then came back laden, put everything away and sat down to a late lunch and then went into the garden and picked forget-me-nots and grape hyacinths and pansies and put a bowl of them in Mrs Vernon's room and another one in the sitting-room and then, after careful thought, hauled the bed away from the wall and moved it so that its head faced the door. Mrs Vernon, lying in bed, would be able to see into the sitting-room through the open door.

Pleased with her efforts, she sat down to make a careful list of her purchases. Mrs Vernon would want to see it when she came.

She was up early the next day. No one had told her at what time they would arrive but she thought it unlikely that they would reach South Pool before the end of the afternoon; she made scones for tea, boiled a small chicken and made broth and then pounded the meat to a cream. She made a jelly and a nice oldfashioned junket and set a tray for tea.

By three o'clock she was ready, very neat in her cotton dress and a cardigan, a brisk little fire in the grate, Mrs Vernon's room nicely warmed.

It was almost five o'clock when the ambulance turned cautiously into the little cul-de-sac. She went out to meet it, looking for another car, but none followed it. Young Mrs Vernon would be inside the ambulance, she supposed, and went to its doors as they were opened.

The district nurse got out first, 'I thought we'd never get here,' she exclaimed to Deborah. 'The old lady has withstood the trip very well, though.'

'You must all be very tired,' said Deborah. 'I thought Mrs Vernon would come too.'

'Not her. Said she wouldn't be able to stand the journey...' The district nurse made a face. 'Is everything ready?'

'Come in and see...' She opened the door wide and ushered the nurse inside and went back to the ambulance. The ambulancemen had the stretcher out now and she bent over Mrs Vernon. 'It's lovely to see you again—and it's a heavenly cottage, isn't it? Come inside and see your room.'

It was surprisingly easy getting her inside and it was simple to get her into bed—although she was tired she was no longer a dead weight. Deborah made her comfortable, promised her a cup of tea and went to the kitchen. 'Tea's ready; you'll all have some, won't you? Would you mind being Mother while I give Mrs Vernon a drink? Should I phone the doctor, do you think?'

'I'll have a good look at her, dear, before we go. Unless there's something not right I should think it would do if you get him out here tomorrow morning. You don't mind being here alone with her?'

'Not a bit.' Deborah added thoughtfully, 'I've always been alone with her, if you see what I mean.'

'Indeed I do. Here are the men—they'll want their tea. You go and see to Mrs Vernon.'

The old lady was very quiet but it was a contented quietness. She held Deborah's hand for a moment and gave it a weak squeeze. When Deborah asked her if she was happy to be there her wink was simply ecstatic and although she could only mumble it was a happy mumble.

The nurse came presently and together they made Mrs Vernon comfortable and the nurse took her blood-pressure and gave it as her opinion that there was nothing to worry about. 'A good night's sleep and get the doctor to see her in the morning, dear.'

'Are you going back this evening?'

'Yes, we must, but we shall stop on the way and have a meal.'

The two men came in then to say goodbye; they were a cheerful pair, cracking mild jokes for the old lady's benefit and patting Deborah on the back in a fatherly fashion. When they had gone the little house was very quiet and within minutes Mrs Vernon had dozed off, which gave Deborah a chance to unpack the case which had come with her and clear away the tea things. She had just finished when the phone rang and she snatched it off the hook as she didn't want to wake Mrs Vernon. It would be young Mrs Vernon, of course...

'Has Mrs Vernon arrived safely?' asked Sir James.

'Oh, it's you, you are kind, how nice,' said Deborah idiotically. 'She came about an hour ago by ambulance. The district nurse came with her.'

'She stood the journey well?'

'Nurse said she had, she checked everything before she went away and told me to get the doctor in the morning.'

'Ah, yes—you did tell me his name...?'

'Did I? It's Wright, he lives at Chillingford—that's the village on the main road.'

Sir James gave a grunt. 'And Mrs Vernon, has she telephoned you yet?'

'No.' She tried to think of something to add to that and couldn't.

'You had better ring her yourself. Have you settled in? You are not nervous?'

'We shall be very comfortable,' said Deborah sedately, 'and I'm not nervous, thank you. It is kind of you to ring.'

'Mrs Vernon is an interesting case. Goodnight, Deborah.'

She hadn't admitted, even to herself, that she was nervous of being alone with the old lady—she was after all still needing a great deal of care and attention—but now Sir James had phoned and she felt all of a sudden perfectly capable of dealing with any situation which might arise. She went to look at Mrs Vernon and found her awake, so she sat down by the bed and told her about Sir James.

Mrs Vernon croaked and grunted and tapped Deborah's hand holding hers. 'Is anything wrong?' asked Deborah.

She had a reassuring wink and another grunt which she liked to think was a laugh.

She phoned young Mrs Vernon presently. 'There was no need to disturb us now,' said that lady. 'Tomorrow morning would have done. Don't telephone us unless it is urgent.'

She hung up before Deborah could ask what she considered urgent.

Dr Wright came in the morning, a young man with a nice face and a friendly manner. Deborah was unaware that Sir James had telephoned him on the previous evening and, after introducing himself and explaining his interest in Mrs Vernon, had suggested that Dr Wright should visit her as soon as possible. 'And I would be most interested to know how she goes on if you should find the time to keep me informed.' Deborah was delighted to see him.

Dr Wright had been more than willing; he had heard of Sir James Marlow, who had attained the peak of his profession, something Dr Wright had every intention of doing himself. He had written down the telephone number he was offered with the promise of keeping Sir James informed at regular intervals and drove to South Pool the next day.

Mrs Vernon had had a good night and was quite ready for him, lying back on her pillows in a fresh nightie and with her hair nicely arranged. She watched him come into the cottage and introduce himself to Deborah before they came through the open door to stand one on each side of her bed.

Nothing would bring beauty to Deborah's ordinary features, but her eyes shone and her skin had the smoothness and perfection of a small child's. Even her hair, released from its restricting bun and tied back with a ribbon, had taken on a softer shade of carrot. Dr Wright thought she looked sensible although he didn't much care for the hair.

He took pains with Mrs Vernon and gave the opinion that after a day or two's rest she might sit on a chair for an hour or two each day. He looked round the room. 'You haven't anything suitable, though . . .'

'If you tell me where I can get the Red Cross I'll borrow one,' said Deborah. 'You mean one of those chairs with a kind of tray in front.'

'That's right, and I should think that in a week or so, if the weather is fine, Mrs Vernon might go out in a wheelchair. I think it might be best if I get the physiotherapy people on to her; massage and exercise and someone to help her with her speech.'

He had a cup of coffee and went away and Deborah sat down and explained everything to Mrs Vernon. 'And he will come again at the end of the week.' She said, 'And by then I think the physio people will have fixed up something.'

She was right. By the end of the first week a nice motherly soul had paid them a visit—Mrs Denny, and she would be coming twice a week for some gentle physio and she would give a hand getting Mrs Vernon out of her bed and into the chair which had arrived with commendable promptitude. Dr Wright had been again, the milkman called each morning and Deborah nipped over to the shop, knowing that the nice plump neighbour would keep an eye on the old lady. Life was unexpectedly fun, although she had no time to herself, only at bedtime when Mrs Vernon, safely asleep, no longer needed her. She should, she supposed, make some plans for the future; Mrs Vernon was making great strides now and once she was no longer completely dependent on other people, she would return to her niece's house, that young Mrs Vernon had made clear to Deborah, and there had been no mention of Deborah going with her, but for the moment she was happy, happier than she had been for a long time, and if now and then she allowed herself to think of Sir James in a wistful fashion she dismissed this with the excuse that she was a bit tired . . .

They had been there for two weeks when Mrs Denny suggested that Deborah might like a few hours to herself. 'There's a good bus to Kingsbridge and it's no distance, and I can take my lunch-hour here as well as anywhere. I'll be here in good time for you to catch the bus in two days' time.'

Deborah had two weeks' wages in her pocket—at least the Vernons' solicitor sent her a regular weekly cheque for food and her wages. She had kept a meticulous account of all the household expenses which she was required to send to him each week, unaware that before long old Mrs Vernon, once she could put pen to paper, would be required to write a cheque to pay for everything.

Kingsbridge was a charming little town, cheerful in the bright spring sunshine, and it was delightful to go from shop to shop, looking in the windows. Seeing a nice café, she had coffee, stocked up on her more mundane necessities and then went in search of something to wear. The things she had were nice enough for daily use but she had nothing fit for any special occasion. That such a thing was likely to happen seemed uncertain, but just supposing Sir James should come to see how Mrs Vernon was getting on; it would be satisfying to her deflated ego if she were looking nice . . .

She found what she had in mind in one of the smart boutiques in the main street: a simple dress of patterned voile in pleasing shades of green and misty blue; it flattered her small waist and pretty figure and although it was more than she had intended to pay she bought it. She bought some sandals too—not sensible ones like she wore every day, but high-heeled trifles which she had to admit she might never wear. And always at the back of her mind was the hope that one day Sir James would come and by some lucky chance she would be wearing them.

One day soon after that he did come, but the lucky chance didn't stretch quite far enough; she was on her knees giving the fireplace a good clean, a pinny wrapped around a cotton dress, bare feet in sensible sandals, her hair tied back and no make-up to speak of on her face. Mrs Vernon's mumbling made her turn round, to find Sir James standing by the door, watching her.

Her feeling of intense pleasure at seeing him was immediately replaced by one of annoyance; she had wanted to be looking her best if and when he did come and here she was looking her very worst. She got slowly to her feet and wished him good morning in a cold voice.

He appeared not to notice that; his 'good morning' was genial and casual. 'I'm on my way to Truro,' he observed blandly. 'It seemed a good opportunity to call and see how Mrs Vernon is progressing.'

'Yes—well, how kind. She's in her chair.' She waved him through the open door. 'I'll get you a cup of coffee—and wash my hands.' She added, 'Mrs Vernon talks a little now and she writes in a notebook.'

She backed out of the room and flew upstairs to take off the pinny, brush her hair and retie it with its ribbon and dash powder over her small nose. Looking at her reflection, she could see that it hadn't made much difference...

When she took the coffee in presently it was to find Mrs Vernon labouring over her notebook and Sir James sitting on the side of the bed, looking very much at his ease. He got up and took the tray from her and pulled up a chair before accepting his mug and a slice of cake.

'The physiotherapist comes, Mrs Vernon tells me— a pleasant person, it seems.' Not giving Deborah time to answer, he continued, 'And Dr Wright?'

He gave her such a long stare that she felt her cheeks go red. 'He comes twice a week,' adding recklessly, 'He's awfully nice; we get on.'

CHAPTER FOUR

DEBORAH wished that she hadn't said that the moment she had; Sir James all of a sudden became a visiting consultant instead of the casual friendly visitor. He said smoothly, 'I'm glad to hear that—you must miss young company here. I'll call and see him presently and in the meantime perhaps I might take a look at Mrs Vernon.'

His impersonal civility hurt her, she supposed because she had come to regard him as a friend. She stood by the bed, where he had laid Mrs Vernon, and watched his intent face as he made a leisurely examination, his large well-kept hands very gentle. Presently he stood upright again.

'Excellent,' he pronounced. 'I dare say Dr Wright will arrange for a wheelchair very shortly. Mrs Vernon is making a splendid recovery.'

He sat down again, listening to her mumbled talk with an encouraging word from time to time, but presently he said goodbye and Deborah went with him to the door.

'You are not tired?' he asked her. 'You have time to yourself? You are a little pale. Are you to return with Mrs Vernon when she goes back to her niece's house?'

'No—well, I don't know, Dr Wright thinks that I should—you see, she's used to me and I can understand her—but I suppose I'll do whatever Dr Benson wants; he'll be in charge again, I imagine?' She peered up at him. 'Not you?' she asked.

'No, no, this was merely a friendly visit. I shall not come again unless I am called in professionally.'

She put out a hand, brown and little and rough with housework. 'Then I'll wish you goodbye, Sir James, and thank you very much.'

He took it into his and held it firmly. 'What will you do if you are no longer needed with Mrs Vernon?'

'Me? Heavens—oh, I shall find another job.' For an appalling instant she visualised the years ahead, going from one job to the next, and dismissed it firmly.

'You will probably marry,' suggested Sir James with remote kindness. 'You would make a good doctor's wife.'

She blushed and he sighed gently; Dr Wright was a nice young chap and Deborah had blushed twice at his name. Sir James wasn't sure why he felt a vague regret. As for Deborah, the blush hadn't been for Dr Wright; she had at that very moment made the discovery that if she were to be a doctor's wife she would want Sir James to be that doctor. Just for the moment nothing and nobody else mattered while she digested this exciting fact before she suppressed it sternly as a load of nonsense.

She wished him goodbye in a quiet little voice and watched him get into his car and drive away. He didn't look at her or wave—all the same, she waited until the Bentley had edged round the corner into the road before going back to Mrs Vernon.

Mrs Vernon looked at her for a long moment, wrote 'sad' on her pad and waited for Deborah to say something.

Deborah shook her head. 'No, no—how nice to see Sir James again, wasn't it? He's very pleased with you; he told me that he found you a very interesting case.'

The old lady nodded slowly. Her wits had never quite deserted her; now they were sharp enough to wonder if the specialist's interest extended to Deborah—not that he realised that, of course. She sighed, a romantic at heart and wishful to see Deborah happy.

Spring had sidled gently into summer and Mrs Vernon was able to do more for herself, walk a few steps with the aid of sticks, even make herself understood when she spoke and was quite happy. Dr Wright came each week and invariably stayed either for coffee or tea and, since he was now on excellent terms with Deborah, his visits were the highlight of their week. As for Deborah, the soft Devonshire air and the wholesome food she cooked had combined to round out her small person in a pleasing fashion and put a healthy colour in her cheeks. Mrs Vernon, studying her serene face, wondered if she was happy. She was always cheerful, ready to talk, and unendingly patient, but there was a wistfulness about her which the old lady found disquieting. It was no life for a young girl, she told Dr Wright while Deborah was getting the coffee; she should be with young people, having a good time. 'I will be sorry if she should ever leave me,' said Mrs Vernon, 'but not, I hope, for the immediate future.'

A hope which was not to be fulfilled. A week later, on a lovely early summer morning as the pair of them sat outside the cottage door, drinking the lemonade Deborah had made, deciding in a desultory manner what they should have for their lunch, a car turned into the cul-de-sac, and Mrs Vernon's nephew and niece got out.

Young Mrs Vernon gave Deborah a brief nod and bent over her aunt. 'We had such an excellent report from Dr Benson—Dr Wright has been sending him a weekly progress report—that we have decided that you are well enough to return home. I have arranged a room for you downstairs and engaged a very good woman to look after you. The garden is quite perfect, you know; you will enjoy sitting there.'

'No,' said her aunt and, because she was deeply disturbed, her speech became muddled and almost unintelligible. Only Deborah understood that she was protesting vigorously and took the matter into her own hands.

No one noticed when she slipped into the cottage and went to the phone. Dr Wright was at home. 'I'll be with you as soon as I can,' he promised and she went outside again.

'Would you like a glass of lemonade or a cup of coffee?'

'Coffee,' said young Mrs Vernon without bothering to look up. 'We'll have it inside.' She looked round the little square of grass. 'I dare say there are several curious neighbours.'

She marched indoors and sat down in the living-room and after a moment her husband wheeled his aunt into the house. Mrs Vernon was silent now but her niece started talking again in a wheedling voice. 'We've bought a wheelchair for you, Aunt; you can go wherever you like. Miss Grant—the woman I've engaged for you—is young and strong and has ex-cellent references.' She broke off as Deborah came in with the coffee and then fetched their glasses of lemonade from the porch. She hadn't said a word, for it seemed there was nothing to be said, but Dr Wright would make the final decision. He came presently, greeted the visitors pleasantly, accepted coffee and sat down beside the old lady.

'Dr Benson tells us that in your opinion my aunt is fit enough to return to my home,' began Mr Vernon a shade pompously. 'Accordingly we have made suitable arrangements—fitted out a room leading on to the terrace, engaged an attendant and bought a wheelchair so that my aunt will feel free to get about.'

Dr Wright saw nothing wrong with this arrangement, merely remarking that he would have preferred to have been told about their plans at an earlier date. 'I presume you do not intend to take Mrs Vernon back with you today? I'm afraid that is something I can't allow. It's a very long journey; she must go by ambulance. I shall also want to examine her very thoroughly first.'

'Naturally. We had no intention of taking Mrs Vernon back with us today. Would you agree to an ambulance fetching her in a few days' time? I will send the attendant with it; she is a very capable young woman.'

'And Deborah?' asked Dr Wright.

'She can stay for a couple of days and close up this place. I'm sure she'll be glad to find another job with younger people.' Young Mrs Vernon glanced at Deborah. 'I'll have your things packed up; the ambulance can bring them when it comes. There's no need for you to come back to us.'

'Does Mrs Vernon want to go?' asked Deborah, speaking at last.

'Of course she wants to be in her own home again; besides, it won't do for her to become too attached to you.' Young Mrs Vernon gave her tinkling laugh. 'We can't have her leaving the family fortune away from the family, can we? I dare say you've done very nicely while you've been here with her.'

She laughed again so that her listeners would think that she was joking but her words fell into a silence broken by Deborah getting to her feet.

'That is an abominable thing to say, Mrs Vernon, and a very vulgar one too. Even if you intended it for a joke...' She stopped, drew a deep breath and went on in a colourless fashion, 'I will have Mrs Vernon ready when the ambulance comes.'

Young Mrs Vernon had gone very red in the face. 'You do that. We will go now. Aunt will want a rest, I dare say, after all the excitement.'

She kissed the old lady's cheek. 'We are so looking forward to having you home again. You will love your room...'

It was Mr Vernon who shook Deborah's hand and thanked her. 'I must apologise for my wife; she sometimes says things she doesn't mean.' He shook Dr Wright's hand too, kissed his aunt and went out to the car and they drove away.

'That was unexpected,' observed Dr Wright. 'I could have wished for a more leisurely approach. Still, the proper arrangements seem to have been made.' He looked at Deborah. 'And although it must be a blow to you, since Mrs Vernon doesn't appear to like you, it may be for the best if you leave now.' He spoke uncertainly but was reassured by Deborah's quiet.

'Oh, I expect it is a splendid arrangement and Mrs Vernon will be happy with a room on the ground floor.' She took the old lady's hand in hers. 'You'll enjoy seeing all your friends again,' she observed cheerfully.

Dr Wright went away presently with the promise that he would return the next day and examine his patient and make sure that she was fit for the journey. It was only after he had gone that the old lady allowed the slow tears to trickle down her cheeks.

Deborah wiped them away. 'You hate the idea of going, don't you?' she said quietly. 'But that's because it's all been rather sudden. We'll have a good talk about it later. Now I'm going out to get our lunch and this afternoon we'll go through the village for a walk and supposing we have one or two of the neighbours to tea tomorrow? They've all been so kind and friendly.'

Mrs Vernon muttered something about something and Deborah fetched her pad and pencil.

'What about you?' wrote Mrs Vernon in her shaky hand.

'I'll stay here for a day or two and close up the cottage then I shall go back to my home for a week or two.'

'Your home?' mumbled Mrs Vernon. 'Mother and Father?'

'Brother and sister,' said Deborah cheerfully, prepared to lie like a trooper to keep the old lady happy. 'We live in Hampstead.' Mrs Vernon looked less upset and she went on, 'Mrs Denny is coming in the morning, isn't she? While she's here I'll pop into Kingsbridge; you need one or two things and so do I.'

She got their lunch and presently pushed Mrs Vernon in her chair round the village, stopping to tell anyone they knew that they would be leaving in the next few days and then going back to the cottage to park Mrs Vernon while she went to invite their few neighbours to tea.

They all came, friendly folk who had been kind and helpful to them both, delighted that Mrs Vernon was well enough to return to her home, assuring Deborah that she would have no trouble finding a job if she needed one.

With an eye on the old lady, Deborah repeated the fiction that she would be going to her home for a few weeks, which drew pleased remarks, for everyone liked her, and the tea party ended in a light-hearted manner.

Dr Wright came directly after morning surgery the next day, pronounced his patient well enough to return home and, on the way out, asked Deborah if she had a job to go to. 'This has all happened rather quickly,' he told her. 'I feel as though I have been the cause of you losing your job. What will you do?'

'I'm going into Kingsbridge when Mrs Denny gets here,' she told him. 'When I was there last I saw several notices in shop windows and at the hotel where I had coffee, all wanting part-time help. I like it here and I thought I'd stay until the summer is over.'

'You have a home to go to?' He sounded concerned so she assured him that she had.

She studied the various notices carefully that afternoon; only one of them offered a live-in job. The hotel was quite small, overlooking the water and a short walk from the centre of the town. It looked pleasant, she decided as she enquired at the reception desk if she could see the manager.

He was elderly and very businesslike and she was equally businesslike, answering his questions in her quiet way, offering Dr Wright's name as a reference, listening attentively as he told her that the work was temporary—six weeks or so, no longer—that she would clean bedrooms, help in the kitchen, sort the laundry, help out wherever it was needed most. She would share a room with the part-time help and he mentioned a wage which seemed to her to be generous. She would have one free day a week too. The working hours, he warned her, would be long.

Provided that Dr Wright's reference was satisfactory she was to start in three days' time. She went back to South Pool with the black bogey of the future pushed out of sight once more. Six weeks would give her time to decide what to do and she would save as much money as she could.

Mrs Vernon was in cheerful mood when she got back and Mrs Denny was still there. Deborah displayed her modest purchases, made tea for the three of them and presently said goodbye to Mrs Denny. The evening was spent packing Mrs Vernon's things while they talked cheerfully enough. Mrs Vernon, now that she had got over the shock of leaving, was more cheerful and inclined to reminisce so that Deborah had to pause from time to time in her packing to sit and listen to her. Speech was still difficult; she only hoped the old lady's new attendant and her friends would be patient...

Young Mrs Vernon phoned that evening; the ambulance would get to the cottage in the early afternoon and Deborah was to have Mrs Vernon quite ready to leave as it would return immediately. Mrs Vernon rang off without saying more.

Deborah was deliberately leisurely in the morning; there was no hurry over breakfast even though it was a little earlier than usual. Mrs Vernon, in a fresh nightie and dressing-gown since they would be the most comfortable garments to wear in the ambulance, was given her morning coffee as usual and settled in a chair while Deborah got an early lunch. She had the kettle on boiling to make a cup of tea when the ambulance crept off the street and stopped before the door.

The ambulancemen were the same pair who had brought them all those weeks ago and the young woman who got out with them was reassuringly friendly with a round open face, and a nice smile.

She shook Mrs Vernon's hand and introduced herself as Maggie and then turned a beaming smile on Deborah. 'What a lovely spot; you'll hate to leave it, but Mrs Vernon says you've a good job to go to. We're supposed to go straight back but I'll be grateful if you could give me some tips...'

'Of course, and the kettle's just boiling—you'll all like a cup of tea?' Fetching the tray, Deborah felt relief that Maggie seemed just the right kind of person to be with the old lady, and probably tough enough to stand up to her niece too.

They had their tea and a talk and presently Deborah took a cheerful leave of Mrs Vernon, promising to write to her, even visit her if she were ever anywhere near the house, and then she watched her stowed carefully in the ambulance and driven away.

She went back into the cottage and sat down on the nearest chair and cried her eyes out. Presently, she got up, mopped her sodden face, cleared away the tea things and began the task of getting the little place ready to close up. She stripped both beds, for the washing and ironing would have to be done before she left; she would sleep between blankets for a couple of nights and do without a tablecloth and napkin. She stowed everything into the washing machine and went to go through the case of clothes which Maggie had brought with her. Everything was there; there hadn't been much anyway.

She spent the rest of the day cleaning and polishing and presently had her supper and went to bed. There would be a lot to do tomorrow and on the following morning after that she was to present herself at the hotel and start work.

She was tired by the time she turned the key in the lock for the last time and went to catch the early morning bus to Kingsbridge. The neighbours had been kind, insisting on giving her supper on the previous evening, offering a bed for the night should she ever need one. She had told them that she had a job to go to but she hadn't said where; now she lugged her two cases to the main street and presently boarded the half-empty bus.

She remembered to go in through the door at the side when she reached the hotel and a rather cross-faced woman who said she was the housekeeper took her to her room and told her to get into the nylon overall and then come downstairs again so that she might be told her duties.

Left alone, Deborah surveyed the room. It was on the top floor with two windows cheaply curtained, two beds at opposite ends of the room, a wardrobe, two chairs and a small table. There was a rug on the floor and a shelf for books. Hardly luxury but very clean and airy. She left her unpacking for later and got into the overall, made sure that her hair was tidy and went back downstairs.

Her duties, she discovered, were manifold; not only did she have her own tasks to perform, she was to take over from other domestic staff whenever they had time off. The housekeeper fixed her with a beady eye. 'You will have a day off in the week, of course. Start work at seven o'clock in the morning, an hour off in the afternoon and off duty at ten o'clock unless you're specially needed.'

Deborah listened meekly. She could see that she would be earning every penny of her wages but that was why she was here, wasn't it? She shouldered the bag which contained dusters and polish, cloths and brushes, and made her way to the bar. The housekeeper would inspect her work at eleven o'clock when she would have ten minutes' break for a cup of coffee.

The girl she shared her room with—Maisie—was a great girl, already inclined to stoutness, but she was disposed to be friendly and by bedtime Deborah was so tired that even Maisie's snores did nothing to disturb her. Her cheerful 'good morning' as she shook Deborah awake was a good start to the day. Deborah scuttled along to the bathroom at the end of the passage and then dressed quickly. There was no need to do anything to her face; she screwed her hair back and, urged by the friendly Maisie, went down to the kitchen. One of the kitchen workers was already there and the three of them shared a pot of tea which gave them the chance to drill Deborah as to her morning duties. They were many and varied but she got through them somehow telling herself that once she had learnt her way around everything would be easier. The guests' breakfasts attended to—trays laid, tea and coffee ready and fresh tea for the cook on duty, then they were free to have their own meal, which meant that Deborah learned that Maisie worked only four days a week. 'So you'll have the room to yourself while I'm at home,' she said. 'Only mind and get yourself an alarm clock,' she warned her.

By the time her free day came, Deborah was almost too tired to enjoy it. Her feet ached with so much running about and although she had settled down into the routine of the hotel it was hard work and the days were over-long. The free time during the afternoon wasn't long enough for her to get to the shops; besides, by then she only wanted to take off her shoes and sit and do nothing.

All the same, she was determined to make the most of her day off. She found a hairdresser who didn't need an appointment and had her fiery hair washed and dried and pinned up by an expert hand and, much cheered by her appearance, she spent time and money choosing lipstick and powder before having coffee and the richest cream cake she could find. Thus fortified, she spent a blissful hour or so peering at the shop windows; she would have liked to have bought some new clothes but with the future so obscure she didn't dare. Perhaps before this job came to an end she would get a skirt and a blouse or two and perhaps a sweater...

She had a meagre lunch presently and then walked along by the estuary before buying dull things like toothpaste and shampoo in Woolworths and then having a splendid tea. There was still the evening, of course, but she had nowhere to go; she bought a packet of biscuits, the local paper and any magazine which might advertise jobs, and went back to her room. Maisie wouldn't be there; she would be going home after her day's work so Deborah had the bathroom to herself, lying far too long in a hot bath and then, in a dressing-gown and nightie, settling down to read and eat the biscuits.

But she didn't read for a long time; she thought about Sir James. Of course she thought of him all day and every day but only in snatches; for most of the time she had so many other things to think of, but now she allowed herself the luxury of remembering everything that she had heard him say, his image vivid in her head. She supposed that in time she would forget him, but at present that was impossible. She thought wistfully that he, of course, would have forgotten her long ago.

She was wrong; he hadn't forgotten her. He supposed it was the carroty head of hair and the bright blue of her eyes which came between him and the book he was reading or the learned notes he was penning. It was a pity, he thought rather testily, that he couldn't spare the time to drive down to South Pool and see how Mrs Vernon was getting on. He had had a couple of reports from Dr Wright—very satisfactory ones too but she was not, after all, his patient, and Dr Benson had said that he would let him know of any drastic change. Presumably sooner or later Deborah and the old lady would return to the niece's house and the dreary room on the top floor. Most unsuitable, he thought frowningly—he could perhaps jog Dr Benson's memory and get a report—— His receptionist interrupted his train of thought then and for the moment he put the idea aside.

Deborah had been at the hotel for almost three weeks when he had a letter from Dr Wright. He had gone early to his consulting-rooms intent on finishing an article he was writing for the *Lancet*, when Mrs Fogg, his receptionist, came in with the post.

'Not much,' she said cheerfully. 'I've taken out the cheques and bills and Mrs Stone phoned to say could she possibly come this morning instead of to-morrow?' Mrs Fogg, who had worked for him for years, added severely, 'You're due at the hospital at noon and you're going to be busy until then.'

Sir James laid down his pen. 'Alice, I don't know what I would do without you. Use your charm to alter Mrs Stone's mind, will you? There is really no need for her to see me again anyway.'

Mrs Fogg didn't say anything. Mrs Stone fancied Sir James, the silly woman. A pity he couldn't find himself a wife—all members of the medical profession needed wives and preferably a brood of children; it put them out of range of tiresome people like Mrs Stone.

'I'll do my best,' she said as she went back to her office.

Left with his letters, Sir James leafed through them idly. The last one was from Kingsbridge.

He opened it and looked at the signature and also saw that it was from Dr Wright before turning to the beginning of it. He read it quickly and then read it again. Dr Wright thought he might like to hear from him, 'Although,' he had written, 'you will already know from Dr Benson that Mrs Vernon is back at her niece's home.' He did add details which he thought might interest Sir James and commented upon the patient's good recovery. He didn't mention Deborah.

Sir James picked up the phone. 'Alice? Get me Dr Benson, will you? You've got his number?'

Mrs Fogg gave a dignified snort. 'Of course, Sir James.' A minute or so later she rang him back. Dr Benson had been ill, a strange voice told him, identifying itself as a Dr Jenkins who had taken over until he was fit again, and how, he enquired, could he help Sir James?

'Yes, indeed,' went on the voice in answer to Sir James's enquiry, he visited a Mrs Vernon, living with a Mr and Mrs Vernon. 'She is making a good recovery and seems both happy and comfortable. She has a splendid attendant who seems quite tireless. Her niece tells me that she doesn't know what they would do without the girl . . .'

'Ah, yes—a small young woman with red hair.'

'No, no—Maggie is a strongly built young woman, dark-haired if I remember rightly. Are you interested in the case? Would you like a full report? Dr Benson will be away for another week or so.'

Sir James said, no, there was no need, he had merely wished to enquire out of personal interest; he added his thanks and hung up. He glanced at his watch— he had five minutes before his first patient. 'Alice? Get me Dr Wright, will you? South Pool—I've no idea of the number or the address.'

Dr Wright sounded cheerful. 'You had my letter, sir? I thought you might be interested to hear the details of the case. Mrs Vernon is a marvellous old lady.'

Sir James agreed gravely, exchanged a few technical details with his colleague and then asked casually, 'The girl looking after her—she returned to her home with Mrs Vernon, I presume? She appeared fond of her.'

'Deborah? No—she had a message from Mrs Vernon's niece to say that they had engaged another attendant who would fetch Mrs Vernon. Deborah stayed behind to close up the cottage. She intended to stay in the area, I believe, and find a job. Sensible young woman.'

Sir James frowned. He made some non-committal remark, expressed the hope that they would meet at some future date, and hung up again. It was nothing to do with him, of course, but he felt uneasy at the idea of Deborah without friends and no particular skills, desperate to find work. 'Probably some ill-paid job with no future to it,' he uttered impatiently, pressing the bell by his desk to warn Mrs Fogg that he was ready for his first patient.

He was far too well disciplined to allow his thoughts to wander until the end of the day, when, his last patient seen, out-patients at the hospital dealt with and a teaching round conducted with his usual calm patience, he got into his car and drove the short distance to his home, a Georgian house in a quiet street conveniently near to Harley Street. Its door was opened as he got out of the car and he was wished good evening by a dour-faced middle-aged man who added gloomily that rain was forecast.

Sir James clapped him on the shoulders as he went past him into the house. 'The farmers will be delighted. Dobbs, I may be going away for a couple of days at the end of the week ... I'll let you know.'

He broke off to repel the advances of a dog who had come bouncing to meet him. 'All right, Bellum, give me five minutes.' He cuffed the dog gently and the beast rolled over, its tongue hanging out. It had a handsome enough muzzle, a long body covered in silky curls and a long plumed tail. As Sir James told his friends who expressed surprise at the sight of the animal, 'His parentage was lost in history.'

The beast led the way now across the hall and into Sir James's study, a comfortable room with a vast partners' desk under its one window, a couple of leather armchairs by the fireplace and a table against one wall housing a word processor and a small filing cabinet.

Sir James sat himself down in the chair behind the desk; he had had a full day and he was tired but he had to decide just what he was going to do. 'The tiresome girl,' he told Bellum, and, 'I dare say she is quite capable of looking after herself.'

Presently he went upstairs with Bellum trotting up the elegant little staircase at his heels, to sit in his bedroom while his master showered and changed. Together they went downstairs again presently into the dining-room where Dobbs served dinner with an air of disapproval and great dignity. Sir James polished off his cheese and got up from the table. 'Please tell Mrs Dobbs that the beef was delicious. What a splendid cook she is.'

Dobbs allowed himself the faintest flicker of a smile. 'That she is, sir. I'll let her know.'

Sir James went to his drawing-room and sat down by the open french window leading to the small walled garden behind the house. It was a pleasant evening and Bellum pranced round the flowerbeds before coming to sit at his feet. Presently Sir James got up and went to his study again and picked up the phone.

'Pat? How are you and Roger and the children? Do you know of anyone who needs help with children or old people or something similar?'

The young woman at the other end of the phone chuckled. 'James, you don't waste a moment in small talk, do you? You won't tell me anything even if I ask but there are one or two things I must know. How old is she, is she trustworthy, does she speak decent English...?'

'Early twenties, I should think, educated, sensible, patient and hard-working.'

'Would you give her a reference?'

'Yes.'

'Then I may be able to help her. Lottie Soames has been landed with a bad-tempered old uncle while the daughter he lived with goes on holiday. You know Lottie, she's almost witless trying to keep him amused and fed. Shall I find out and let you know?'

'Please—as soon as possible.'

'I am a good sister,' said the voice, and then before saying goodbye, 'Is she pretty, James?'

'Carroty hair and no looks worth mentioning.' He put down the phone.

'However, she has the most beautiful eyes,' he told Bellum, and got out his appointments book.

He left his house very early on Saturday morning with Bellum sitting beside him and Dobbs' gloomy forebodings about bad weather ringing in his ears. Once clear of the city, he drove steadily, stopping for coffee and then for a late lunch, unhampered by much traffic for most of it was going away from the holiday area now that summer was coming to a close. He reached South Pool in the early afternoon and turned the car into the cul-de-sac, to stop before the cottage door. The jolly woman who lived next door was on the doorstep before he could get out.

'They've gone—you've been here before, haven't you? Been gone more than three weeks. A crying shame if you ask me, leaving that nice little thing on her own like that—the old lady was that upset.'

Sir James opened the door to let Bellum out. 'Did Deborah say where she was going?'

'No, only packed the place up like she was told to do and went to Kingsbridge on the bus, said something about starting work in the afternoon.' She paused. 'Wait a minute, though, Mrs Croft on the other side said she thought she saw her polishing the brass on the door of one of the hotels.' She gave Sir James a thoughtful look. 'Want to see her, do you?' When he nodded in his calm way she added, 'Come over and see if she's in.'

Mrs Croft was quite sure that it had been Deborah. 'The hair, you know,' she observed. 'Last week it was; I'd gone in on the early bus and there she was. It's a small hotel facing the water—you can't miss it.'

'You have been most helpful and I am grateful,' said Sir James at his most urbane.

'Well, she surely could do with a few friends, I reckon,' said the jolly woman. 'Like a cup of tea?'

'I should like to see Deborah as soon as possible, but perhaps another time?'

He got into the car and Bellum arranged himself beside him.

'There's a gent for you,' said Mrs Croft as he drove away.

CHAPTER FIVE

Sir James stood in the doorway of the hotel's bar and watched Deborah polishing glasses. She was standing on a chair, since the heavy shelf was too high for her to reach, and showing a great deal of leg. He admired her for a few moments before he spoke, his voice carefully casual.

'What a tiresome girl you are, disappearing without trace, not telling a soul where you were going.'

Deborah, taken by surprise, teetered on the chair and he strode forward and lifted her down, took the glass from her hand and put it on the bar.

'I might have smashed that glass,' she said crossly. 'They take breakages out of our wages.' She wasn't going to allow the pure joy at seeing him again to show. 'Why should I tell anyone where I was going?'

She backed away a little, for standing close to him was doing things to her breath, and, since he had remained silent, she added, 'Did you want to stay here? The receptionist has gone to tea. I'll fetch her.'

'I haven't come to stay.' He smiled at her, a warm friendly smile which did her heart good. 'I have been asked to find you and offer you a job—a friend of my sister's. I must say,' he went on testily, 'that I have spent the better part of two days looking for you.'

'I am working here,' said Deborah with dignity.

'Scullerymaid? Daily help?' He was mocking her and that hurt.

'I'm a chambermaid and I—I help out when any-one's off duty...'

He eyed her silently for a moment. She looked rather bedraggled in a serviceable apron, much too large for her, with a face devoid of make-up and a hairdo like a crow's nest. He thought with impatience that he had no reason to bother with her, she had found work; she looked forlorn but that would be remedied if she combed her hair and did something to her face. No doubt she would work her way up to whatever job was top of the pile in hotels. He had been concerned for her unnecessarily.

She put up a hand and pushed a carroty curl behind one ear and he realised that he was still concerned.

'This job—if you can spare a minute? A friend of my sister's—she has a great-uncle living with her—in his eighties and a little eccentric. She has two small children and a large house and needs help badly. I might add that she is not in the least like Mrs Vernon. Her name is Lottie Soames, in her early thirties, these small children and a good-natured husband. There's plenty of help in the house, you wouldn't be expected to—er—polish glasses.'

To Deborah, already tired and with the rather daunting prospect of a long evening's work ahead of her, it sounded like heaven. 'But I can't just leave...'

'Temporary, are you?' And when she nodded, he said, 'Will you leave that to me and go to Lottie? She really is beside herself, she's a darling but not very well organised.'

'He'll never let me go...'

Sir James smiled. 'Where is this man? The manager, is he?'

'He'll be in his office. It's down that passage by the reception desk.'

Deborah had finished the glasses and was polishing the bar counter when Sir James returned. 'That's settled,' he said blandly. 'How long will it take you to pack your things?'

'Pack my things?' She stared at him, her mouth half open.

He looked at his watch. 'Half an hour? I'll wait here.'

'Yes, but I'm only halfway through the week—I'm supposed to give a week's notice, I can't just go...'

'Indeed you can; the manager was most understanding.'

'What did you say to him?'

He gave a small smile. 'Run along and pack and do take off that terrible pinny.'

She went, for there seemed that there was nothing else that she could do, and half an hour later, neat and tidy once more in the denim skirt and the jacket, she went back to the bar. Sir James and the manager were sitting together on the best of terms. They both turned to look at her as she crossed the bar and Sir James got up.

'I am most grateful for your understanding,' he told the manager. 'You have been most kind.'

The men shook hands and the manager bade Deborah goodbye in quite a different kind of voice from the one he usually used. He sounded sympathetic and slightly deferential too, which puzzled her, but Sir James whisked her out of the hotel so fast that she had no time to ponder upon that.

He opened the door of the car and told her briskly to get in while he saw to her cases, and Bellum, delighted to have company again, stood up on his hind

legs and breathed all over her before Sir James got
him out of the car and walked him briskly up and
down for a few minutes. It gave her a moment in
which to think and she was ready with her questions
as he got back into the car.

'Where are we going and where does this Mrs
Soames live and how do you know I'll suit?'

He started the car before he replied. 'We are going
to my sister's home, that is near Bradford-on-Avon;
you will spend the night there and in the morning she
will drive you over to Lottie who lives just outside
Chippenham.'

'Supposing I decide not to go? I've been hustled
and bustled.' She drew an exasperated breath.

He had driven out of the town and was already on
the road to Totnes.

'Is it not a little late to change your mind?' he asked
mildly.

'Change my mind? I wasn't given a chance to—
to...'

'Now, now.' His voice was very soothing. 'What
would you have done in a few weeks' time when the
job at the hotel was finished? Found more temporary
work? Answered endless advertisements, gone on the
dole? You must admit that it was providential that
my sister should ask me if I knew of anyone who might
go to Lottie and that reminded me of old Mrs Vernon
and you. I dare say Lottie's uncle is rather more difficult to handle.'

She reflected with a touch of melancholy that she
seemed fated to look after old people in their beds.
But at least she would have a roof over her head and
she had been secretly worrying about what she should
do when the hotel no longer needed her services; it

was indeed providential that Sir James's sister should have mentioned this old uncle . . .

Sir James, watching her out of the corner of his eye, was satisfied that his slight deviation from the truth had settled the matter. He began to tell her the latest news of old Mrs Vernon—doing very nicely and when he had seen her recently she had asked after Deborah. 'She is apparently quite fond of the girl who is with her now, but she remembers you with real affection.'

'I'm glad she's better—they're kind to her?' She sounded anxious.

'Oh, yes.' His voice was dry. 'When she dies her nephew and niece will inherit the house and the estate. I hear that when she returned to them she indicated that unless she was allowed to deal with her own affairs she might consider leaving everything to some charity or other.'

'Oh, good. They were unkind to her, but you see they didn't expect her to recover.'

'Common error, that. It is largely due to you that she made a good recovery. Let us hope that you will work wonders with this great-uncle of Lottie's.'

They were racing towards Exeter and Deborah longed for her tea. The staff lunch, although adequate, had to be eaten quickly and if one were interrupted for any reason there was no chance of finishing the meal. She had been interrupted at lunch—twice.

She saw a Happy Eater as they approached the city but Sir James didn't stop; they were on the other side of Exeter, halfway to Honiton when he stopped outside a hotel by the side of the road.

'Tea?' He sounded friendly. 'Go on in while I see to Bellum.'

He opened the door for her and then bent to put a lead on Bellum and she went inside. It was pleasantly warm with a bright fire and comfortable chairs round small tables. First, though, the Ladies'—plenty of hot water and large mirrors and time to see her face. Her hair looked awful too. She did the best she could and went back to find him already at a table with Bellum sitting on his feet. He got up and pulled out a chair, offering it to her, and Bellum arranged himself between them.

'Oh, I ordered—you don't mind? Tea, toasted tea-cakes and a dish of pastries.'

They didn't linger over the meal and Deborah, her head full of questions, forbore from asking them because she sensed that he had no time to waste. He drove on, keeping to the A303 until he came to the fork, when he turned on to the A37, going north now to Midsomer Norton and then, by a series of country roads, to Bradford-on-Avon. Just short of the town he turned into a lane leading into a wooded valley and a half-hidden village. It had one street, a large church and at its end a rambling old house set in a splendid garden.

Sir James drove through the open gateway. 'Well, here we are.' And as he spoke the door was flung wide and a young woman came running out.

She stuck her head through the window and kissed his cheek. 'James—come inside . . .' She leaned across him and offered a hand. 'Hello, Miss Everett—you've no idea what an angel you're being. You don't mind spending the night here? It's a bit too late to take you over to Lottie's. We can go after breakfast.'

She was very like her brother, thought Deborah; the same fair hair and blue eyes and same commanding nose, softened into feminine lines. She took the hand and murmured and Sir James got out of the car and came round to her door and opened it for her.

'You'll stay for dinner?' asked his sister as she ushered them into the house. 'The children are in bed but they've vowed they'd stay awake until you came.'

'I can't stay, my dear, I've a date. But I'll go and see the children—will I?—while you take Deborah to her room. Is Roger home?'

'He went down to the paddock to see Queenie; he'll be back.' She paused to look at him. 'Your date's a bit late in the evening, isn't it? It'll take you two hours and you'll have to change, I suppose.'

'Supper—I should also have gone to the opera too but I cried off.'

'Is she beautiful and charming?' Pat laughed up at him.

All he said was, 'Don't fish, my dear.'

Deborah, who had been feeling pleased with herself for ignoring her feelings and pretending that she didn't love him—it had been a flash in the pan, she had repeated over and over to herself—knew that it was no such thing; she felt quite sick at the idea of him sharing his evening with some lovely, elegant creature. A kind of cold despair filled her chest and just for a moment life just wasn't worth living. It only lasted for a moment; Sir James whistled to Bellum and took the stairs two at a time and his sister took Deborah's arm.

'I don't know your name,' said Deborah.

'Pat—and my husband is Roger—Cresswell. Come on upstairs and see your room. You must be tired.

James said there would be no trouble arranging for you to leave your job...'

Deborah let that pass. He hadn't known where she was in the first place and, now she came to think of it, what had he said to the hotel manager? She would have to ask him...but she wouldn't be seeing him again.

Her room was at the end of a passage leading from the gallery which circled the staircase. It was charming and she heaved a sigh of pure content at the sight of its pretty furnishings and the small bathroom leading from it.

'Don't bother to change,' said Mrs Cresswell. 'We aren't going to—come down as soon as you're ready. Dinner will be in about fifteen minutes.'

When she got downstairs Sir James, his sister and another man were standing in the hall with Bellum pressed close to his master's trouser leg. As Deborah reached them Sir James said, 'I'm sorry I have to go again but I know you will be happy with Lottie, despite her great-uncle. I have rushed you around rather, haven't I?' He smiled down at her as he offered her a hand.

'A bit,' she said composedly, 'but I'm most grateful to you and I'll do my best.' She met his searching look with an effort. 'Thank you for the lift here; I enjoyed it.'

Driving away presently, Sir James was rather surprised to find that he had enjoyed it too. 'That should see her settled,' he observed to Bellum, sitting beside him. 'Probably she will meet some young man and marry.'

The thought of a secure future for the tiresome girl should have left him satisfied but it didn't.

The Cresswells were kindness itself to Deborah, taking care not to ask questions, discussing the delights of Devonshire and their horror of living in a city, the naughtiness of their two children, their garden . . . and sitting her down to a meal the like of which she hadn't enjoyed for a long time. 'And since we are celebrating Lottie's relief at getting you—rather like manna from heaven, you know—we'll have a bottle of champagne.'

Deborah went to bed in a state of slightly muzzy contentment. All the same she wasn't so muzzy that she was unable to go over the hours she had spent with Sir James. It really was the last time, she decided. She wasn't sure why he had bothered to go to so much trouble to find her and get her another job but she suspected that she had nagged at him like a sore tooth. He wasn't a man to leave a stray animal out in the rain and probably that was what he thought of her. It did nothing for her ego—if she thought about it too much she would start wallowing in self-pity. She sensibly went to sleep.

Breakfast was a cheerful meal with the children, a boy and a girl, full of curiosity and questions while being urged to eat their breakfast. 'Roger drops them off on his way to the office,' explained Pat. 'They both go to the same little prep school at present. Paul is down for Winchester of course because Roger went there but Molly will be a day pupil—there's a good school in Bath.'

After the children and their father had gone they sat over their coffee until Pat said, 'Well, if you're ready, Deborah, we'll go over to Lottie's.'

Half an hour took them to Chippenham. Pat drove through the town and took a small side-road. 'Lottie lives right in the country but it's not as bad as it sounds—it's easy to get on to the Marlborough road or go north and pick up the M4. James shoots up to town from us in no time at all.'

She took an even narrower road at the crossroads and drove between high hedges until there was a sharp curve revealing a village ahead of them. There was one very small shop and a cluster of cottages and then they were between hedges again, but not for long. Pat turned into an open driveway leading to a solid house with an elaborate porch and rows of windows set in its plain face. The grounds around it were beautiful and well kept.

'Come along,' said Pat and slipped an arm through Deborah's. 'Don't be nervous; everyone loves Lottie.'

Deborah wasn't surprised about that as she was introduced to that lady who had come tearing out of the door, talking as she came.

'Pat, darling—you angel—and dear James taking all this trouble——'

She turned to Deborah and held out a hand. 'You have no idea just how thankful I am to see you, Miss . . . no, may I call you Deborah? Probably you'll not want to stay once you've met Uncle Oscar, but do please give us a try. I hope I've done the right thing—I thought we'd surprise him with you . . .' She urged them both into the house. 'There's coffee in the sitting-room. I'll tell you all about it, Deborah, before you meet him.'

'He sounds like an ogre.'

'He's an old tyrant. It's his best hobby to find fault with everything and everyone but actually I suspect that he's rather a nice old thing underneath. I'd not seen him for years, you know, but my cousin simply had to have a holiday and now the doctor says she must have three months or so doing nothing and he's been here less than three weeks and I'm half dead . . .'

She smiled brilliantly at Deborah. She was a pretty young woman and obviously, despite her awkward relative, a happy one. She was dressed carelessly but her clothes were expensive and she wore them with an air. Deborah hoped—cautiously—that she would like her.

'Have another cup of coffee while I tell you your duties—you'll have a day off each week, of course, and you can, if you prevail on Uncle Oscar, have several hours off each day. There's no nursing—he's as fit as a fiddle—but he likes to play two-handed patience and bezique and talk—he reminisces by the hour. You'll need an awful lot of patience . . .'

She eyed Deborah doubtfully. 'It sounds awful, doesn't it? But we'll do all we can to keep you happy. I almost forgot,' she added, 'we thought about your salary.' She named a sum which made Deborah blink.

'That's far too much, Mrs Soames . . .'

'Well, you'll have to argue with Peter about that but I assure you that he won't listen and you'll earn every penny of it. If you hadn't come he'd have had to pay hundreds of pounds to some discreet home where I could go mad in comfort.'

They all laughed then and Pat got up to go. Mrs Soames went out to the door with her and when she was in the car poked her head through the window.

'She's sweet—no looks but lovely eyes. She looks sad . . . where did James find her?'

Pat told her. 'I rather gather that he felt responsible for her . . .'

They exchanged a look. 'I'll have him over to dinner one evening,' said Lottie. 'I'll give you a ring in the morning.'

'You shall see your room now,' she told Deborah when she went back into the large, comfortable and untidy sitting-room, 'then you can unpack and come back here and we'll go and surprise Uncle Oscar.'

The staircase was oak and uncarpeted and beautifully polished and upstairs there were passages in all directions. Deborah's room was at the side of the house with a glorious view of the countryside. It was well furnished and there was an easy-chair by the little table under the window. There were books too and a bowl of flowers. Deborah felt tears in her eyes at so much kindness. 'It's beautiful,' she told Mrs Soames. 'I'm sure I shall be happy here and I'll do my best to keep your uncle happy.'

'I'm sure you will. Here's the bathroom and if you need anything do ask. We've a housekeeper and a splendid housemaid and daily help and they'll do all they can to make you comfortable. I'll leave you while you unpack, shall I?'

She went away and Deborah sat down for a moment in the easy-chair. Even if Great-Uncle Oscar was a troublesome tyrant, she would still have time to herself before she went to bed, to sit here and browse through some of the books. She allowed herself to think of the money she would earn too—about three months, Mrs Soames had said. She would save at least half of it so that if she had difficulty in finding work she could rent a room somewhere.

She got up and unpacked, laying undies in the big chest of drawers against one wall and hanging her few clothes in the wall cupboard. She would have to get another dress ...

Hair brushed, and nicely made-up, she went downstairs and found Mrs Soames waiting for her.

'He's along here.' She led the way along a wide corridor. 'A bedroom and sitting-room—there's a door into the garden; he likes gardens—my mother lived with us until she died and we furnished the rooms for her. Of course he uses the other rooms; has his meals with us unless he decides he doesn't want to, often spends the evening watching television and talking loudly all the time. He won't have it in his room but he has got the radio. He comes with us to church but he doesn't like the children much and he loves his solitude.' Mrs Soames paused with her hand on a door-handle and knocked.

A voice thundered, 'Come in,' and she opened the door and encouraged Deborah with a hand on the small of her back.

'Morning, Uncle,' she said cheerfully, and started to cross the floor of the room. It was a large apartment, very well furnished, its windows overlooking a rose garden, its doors open on to a patio. The old gentleman was sitting by the door, and facing away from them—all Deborah could see was a shock of white hair and an upraised newspaper.

He spoke testily without looking round. 'Can I not be left in peace for more than ten minutes at a time? Now what is it?'

His niece went to stand in front of him, taking Deborah with her.

'This is Deborah; she's going to stay with us and be your companion.'

A cross old face emerged from behind the newspaper. 'Companion? Did I ever say I wanted one? Send her away—you're here to give me a game of cards when I want a change.'

'Well, I'm not—not any more,' said Lottie with spirit. 'I've the house to run and the children and Roger to look after. Now you'll have Deborah to help you with the crossword puzzles and play cards with you.'

He put down the paper slowly and took a good look. 'Good lord, she's a child—no use to me at all.'

'Well, supposing you give me a try for a while before you decide,' said Deborah quite unimpressed by this show of rudeness. She had after all, had a good deal of experience of that. 'How do you do, Mr...? I'm afraid I don't know your name.' She held out a hand and he took it reluctantly.

'God bless my soul,' he observed, 'you've a tongue in your head. My name is Trent.'

'Appearances are deceptive,' said Deborah matter-of-factly. 'Never mind what I look like, I'm good at crossword puzzles and I can play most card games. I can play chess, too, Mr Trent.'

'I don't believe it.'

She gave him a smiling look. 'Try me. This afternoon, perhaps?'

'You're a plain girl but you seem to have your wits about you. We'll start a game after lunch. You'll be at lunch?'

'Of course she will,' said Mrs Soames. 'One o'clock, sharp. Come along, Deborah, you'd better see the house and meet the staff.'

It was a delightful house and the housekeeper and Edith the housemaid were softly spoken country-

women who smiled at her kindly. There was an elderly
woman washing up at the sink too, wearing an old
and rather grand hat and a floral pinny, Mrs Hewish
by name, who peered at Deborah and said, 'Ullo,
love,' in a gruff friendly voice.

As they went back to the sitting-room the phone
rang and Mrs Soames went to answer it. 'Take a quick
look round the garden,' she told Deborah and, when
she had gone, lifted the receiver.

'I knew it was you, James. You don't have to worry
about your lame dog—not that that's right but you
know what I mean. You should have seen her with
Uncle Oscar—challenged him to a game of chess after
lunch and when he was rude to her merely said that
appearances were deceptive and told him not to mind
what she looked like. She's a treasure. You won't need
to bother about her any more, I'll see that she gets a
good job when she goes from here; better still I'll see
that she meets as many young men as I can lay hands
on...'

A light-hearted remark which made Sir James frown
thoughtfully. All he said was, 'I'm glad that she's settling in; she hasn't had much fun for the last few
years.'

'Well, we'll try and alter that; Uncle Oscar's going
to take up a good deal of her day but there'll be time
over for some fun.'

Sir James frowned again and then reminded himself
that he had no reason to feel annoyance at Lottie's
remarks. Deborah had as much right to fun, whatever
that was, as any other girl who had to work for her
living.

Sitting at his desk presently, he decided that he
might take a weekend off and go down and see Pat

and call on Lottie at the same time. His nurse came in to say that his first patient was there and he dismissed Deborah from his mind. On his way to the hospital later that morning he paused by Mrs Fogg's desk.

'Alice, I'm going to take a weekend off within the next week or so. How am I fixed?'

She had the appointments book open. 'Let's see. It's Thursday today. This weekend's no good—the conference—you're speaking too. The weekend after that—let me see—you've accepted an invitation to spend Sunday with Dr Frobisher and his wife. The following weekend is free...'

'Good. Remind me, Alice; I'll go to the cottage first so try and keep Friday late afternoon free and first thing Monday morning if you can. I'll be at the hospital if you want me. I'll be back for the afternoon patients.'

'Please don't forget your evening clinic, Sir James.'

She watched him go through the door. It was high time he had a wife to look after him; Dobbs and Mrs Dobbs were splendid servants but what he needed was a loving woman to nag him into a less busy life.

Deborah was very much on her mettle. She got out the chessboard and set it on the table by the window, convenient to Uncle Oscar's chair. Lunch had been a delicious meal, spoilt by his grumblings and criticism of the food put before him. No wonder Mrs Soames had threatened to go into a quiet home and go mad, but, as Deborah told herself, she was made of sterner stuff; moreover she had no other responsibilities and she was being paid handsomely. She set out the pieces and sat down opposite the old gentleman.

He might be crotchety and rude but he certainly had retained his sharp brain. She wasn't bad herself; endless games with a fault-finding stepfather had perfected her game and Uncle Oscar was good enough to tell her that for a chit of a girl she seemed to have a modicum of sense. 'More than Lottie has,' he declared. 'More hair than wit is my opinion of her.'

'Mr Trent, I won't sit here and listen to you saying nasty things about Mrs Soames; she's kind and sweet to you and you know you don't mean a word of it.'

'Hoity-toity, miss, that's no way to talk to your betters. I am ready for tea.'

'So am I,' said Deborah equably. 'Shall I go and look for it or do you have it with Mrs Soames?'

Uncle Oscar blew his nose furiously with a very large handkerchief. 'If we're speaking we have it together but go and tell her I want my tea here; we'll have another game before dinner.'

Deborah found Mrs Soames lolling on a sofa, reading a book. The room was pleasantly untidy and a small dog shared the sofa with her. She looked up guiltily as Deborah knocked and went in. 'Oh, dear— I feel guilty sitting here and doing nothing. Can't you bear him any longer?'

Deborah chuckled. 'We've had a very pleasant afternoon and I'm sure you deserve every minute of peace, Mrs Soames. Mr Trent wants his tea and I wondered if I could get it? He'd like another game of chess afterwards so he'd like it in his room.'

Mrs Soames let out a sigh of relief, 'You have no idea—well, you must have by now—but if he has tea in his room it means the children can rush about and shout and let off steam; I'm going to fetch them in ten minutes or so. I'm sure he's fond of them but they are tiring... Would you go to the kitchen and ask for tea to be taken to Uncle's room? You don't mind having it with him? He goes to bed quite early...' Mrs Soames looked so anxious that Deborah hastened to assure her that she would like to have tea with the old gentleman and went off to the kitchen where Faith offered to bring the tray in five minutes.

Uncle Oscar beat Deborah soundly in the second game and then stumped away to his bedroom to get ready for dinner. 'And you come back here in half an hour,' he told her.

She supposed that she had better wear the new dress. She showered and got into the dress and sandals and brushed her hair into a glossy knot pinned high on her neck and then went back to his room. He was there in his shirt-sleeves, a velvet jacket over his arm.

'Why is there never anyone to help me when I need to be helped?' he greeted her. She saw that it was a routine grumble and meant nothing much. She eased him into the plum-coloured velvet, told him he looked very handsome, and as the gong sounded just then, went with him through the house to the dining-room, a magnificent opulent room with a long table capable of seating twenty persons, ringed by Georgian chairs and set with lace-edged mats and a great deal of glass and silver. She was glad she was wearing the new dress, for Mrs Soames was in a white chiffon blouse and a black taffeta skirt...

The meal went off very well. Uncle Oscar objected to almost everything, the food was badly cooked, the conversation dull and the children had been making a lot of noise.

'They're children, Uncle,' his nephew pointed out mildly, 'and anyway, there is no need to upset yourself, they are in bed now. I've just been up to say goodnight.'

'Bah,' said Uncle Oscar. 'I was brought up to be seen and not heard.'

A remark which was received in silence, the obvious unspoken answer hanging heavy in the air above them.

Over dessert he said suddenly. 'Can you play the piano, miss?'

'Yes,' said Deborah, 'but not very well.'

'There is a piano in my room, you can play for me for half an hour.'

Deborah took a mouthful of peach melba; she said serenely, 'Very well, Mr Trent.'

'Deborah has had a long day,' Mrs Soames pointed out. 'Perhaps she would like to go to bed early.'

'Go to bed?' rumbled her uncle. 'At her age? Good lord, when I was young I was never in bed before two o'clock.'

To her surprise he turned to Deborah. 'Tired, are you?'

'A little, but I shall enjoy playing for a while, Mr Trent.'

They went back to his sitting-room presently and she sat down at the piano at one end of the room and asked him what he would like.

'Anything, anything,' he told her testily, so she rambled from Schubert to Chopin and Elgar and Grieg and then, since he hadn't complained so far, started on some of the old ballads, ending with 'Come into the garden, Maud'.

'Upon my soul,' said Uncle Oscar, 'that was the best half-hour of the day.' He sounded quite mild.

'Go to bed, girl, and send that woman—what's her name? Edith—to run my bath. I'm going to bed too.'

She bade him goodnight and went in search of the housemaid to give her the message and then went to her room. She didn't suppose that the Soameses would expect her to say goodnight.

She was tired but the warm room was wonderfully welcoming with the curtains drawn and the bed turned tidily down. There was a bowl of fruit on the table too. She lay a long time in the bath, eating an apple, recalling the day. It had been a busy one but she liked Uncle Oscar; his bark, she decided, was worse than his bite. In bed, however, the last person she thought of was Sir James. Strangely enough, he was thinking of her too, but whereas she was thinking of him with love and longing his thoughts were impatient of his inability to forget her. It was the hair, he supposed irritably; it had been the first thing he had seen when he had been called to see old Mrs Vernon. It had lighted that bleak room, taking its colour from the daffodils there. 'Tiresome girl,' observed Sir James to the faithful Bellum. 'Let us forget her and concentrate on the dinner party tomorrow evening.'

CHAPTER SIX

UNLIKE old Mrs Vernon, Uncle Oscar was neither supine nor patient. Despite his age he was constantly seeking diversions of one sort or another. Since he was also forgetful and might take a fit into his head to walk to the village and get on a bus for no reason at all, or spend a morning in the garden wreaking havoc among the flower beds, cutting bunches of roses and eating the raspberries, Deborah soon understood why his niece had been so anxious to get help. All the same, she was happy; no two days were alike, for she never knew what Uncle Oscar would do next, so that she might spend almost all of one day playing racing demon with him and the next strolling down to the village shop with him because he fancied a bag of humbugs. They would walk back to the house, their cheeks bulging, and she would stop deliberately from time to time because he was puffing and getting tired, and ask him to tell her about some flower or other.

She had almost no time to herself but she didn't mind that—the Soameses were kind and friendly and the two children were delightful; naughty and noisy and wilful but never disagreeable. She thought how wonderful it must be to be married, like Lottie, to a man who obviously loved her dearly, and to have two healthy and lively children and to live in a lovely house with enough money.

Uncle Oscar liked her; he was rude, of course, but she knew that he didn't mean it. He would bellow and rage at her because she refused even to let him climb up the church tower or ride the postman's bicycle, call her names and then roar with laughter. She found him delightful even if rather a responsibility.

On her first day off Mr Soames drove her into Chippenham in the morning and she spent a most satisfactory day going round the shops and, since she had money to spend, buying another dress to wear in the evenings: a rather sober dress, pale grey with a white ruffled collar and white cuffs to its long sleeves. Suitable, she considered, for any future job she might find, its style vague enough to last through several summers if necessary.

She had lunch in a small restaurant in a side street and, obedient to Mr Soames's request, was waiting for him when he picked her up just before six o'clock.

She found Uncle Oscar in a rage. 'Where have you been?' he bawled as she went into the sitting-room. 'The fools have lost my reading spectacles and Lottie doesn't know a pawn from a knight. I'm upset and I need a drink.'

'You know quite well that it's my day off,' said Deborah soothingly, 'and I can see your glasses from here, they're hanging out of your jacket pocket. We'll have a game of chess before I go to bed if you like and I'll fetch you a drink if you'll say what you want.'

She put the glasses on his nose, invited him to sit quietly and went away to get him the glass of sherry he enjoyed before dinner. That done, she went to her room and changed into the green patterned dress once more. Tomorrow she would wear the new frock.

Another week went by; summer was ending and although there was not any mention of her leaving she hoped that it wouldn't be for at least another two months. By then she would have enough money saved to keep her while she found work; all the same she worried quietly to herself, getting ready for bed in her pretty room.

On the Saturday morning, Uncle Oscar declared his intention of walking to the village to buy sweets. It was a grey cool morning and it was already drizzling with a fine rain but since he had made up his mind the pair of them set out, Deborah holding aloft an enormous umbrella. The village shop was crowded and when their turn came the old gentleman took time deciding what he would have. Presently, however, his pockets bulging with toffees and striped humbugs, they set off for the house once more. Despite the rain, which was now quite hard, they didn't hurry, for he was in a chatty mood and kept stopping to explain some knotty point to Deborah. They were halfway up the drive when she looked up and saw the Bentley on the sweep before the house.

'Oh, lord!' said Deborah and stopped short.

Her companion squinted through the rain. 'That's James's car. Why are you standing there like a thunderstruck goose? Seen him before, haven't you? Nice chap, clever too.' He gave her a sly look. 'Sweet on him, are you? Shouldn't be surprised; he's a good catch, not that he'd notice you with that hair. Lottie said something about his help in finding you—he's always been a one to find homes for stray cats and dogs.'

Deborah spoke coldly. 'Mr Trent, you are a vulgar and rude old man and I know you don't mean half of it.'

He took this in good part. 'I like a bit of temper in a woman,' he told her and took her arm. 'Let us go and say good morning to James.'

He started to walk towards the house and she perforce went with him because of the umbrella, but at the door she said quickly, 'I must go to the kitchen and see about your coffee. Mind and change your shoes and put on your slippers.'

She skipped away and Sir James watched her go from the drawing-room window. She looked as plain as ever, he reflected, her hair wet and curling fiercely around her face, and yet he felt distinct pleasure in seeing her again.

He asked idly, 'Deborah has settled down nicely, Lottie?'

'She's a gem, she takes the greatest care of Uncle Oscar, ignores his bad temper and rudeness and spends hours playing chess with him. We are so grateful for her. Madeleine won't recognise him when she gets back.'

'When is she returning?'

'I'm not sure, a while yet. Deborah must be longing to get back to her normal life again. Her family must miss her.'

'She has no family—stepbrother and sister...'

'Oh, I didn't know. She doesn't talk about herself at all.' She smiled at him. 'Come and sit down and tell me what you've been doing lately. Pat says you are far too busy.'

'I intend to have a quiet weekend. It seemed a good opportunity to call and see if Deborah was fitting in...'

'Indeed she is. We feel a bit guilty, though, she doesn't get much free time: a day—most of a day—

once a week; she goes to Chippenham and looks at the shops.'

Sir James, very relaxed in his chair, crossed one long leg over the other. 'I'll ask her out to dinner—tomorrow evening?'

'What a marvellous idea, I'm sure she'll love that. Go and ask her now. She'll be giving Uncle Oscar his coffee in his sitting-room. Pat's coming over for tea and bringing the children—will you come too?'

'I'd like to spend the rest of the day at the cottage, and tidy up the garden a little.'

'Of course. Come when you like, though, James, you're always welcome. Do see Peter before you go—he'll be down in the paddock with the children. I suppose that's where Bellum went . . .'

'I'll give him a whistle and see Uncle Oscar on the way.'

Sir James reached Uncle Oscar's door at the same time as Deborah, coming from the kitchen with the coffee tray. He took it from her, wished her 'good morning' in a civil voice and followed her into the room.

'Thought you'd come,' observed the old man. 'Where's that ridiculous dog of yours? Come to talk to me, have you? Deborah, pour the coffee and get another cup and saucer. Want to see how she's coping with me, do you?'

He turned his elderly gaze upon her and she took no notice, merely poured the coffee with a steady hand, steeling herself for whatever he would say next. Which was a good thing, for the old man went on loudly, 'No glamour but as wholesome as a loaf of bread, and she plays an excellent game of chess and you get used to the hair.'

Sir James's face was expressionless; he said pleasantly, 'You can hardly expect me to agree with you, sir, but I am pleased to hear that Deborah is still here despite your—er—forthright comments.'

He reached for the coffee-cup she was holding out to him and saw that her hand was trembling. He took the cup and with his other hand held hers for a moment, its grasp firm and warm. He said with casual friendliness, 'I've given myself a weekend off. I'd like to take you out tomorrow evening—dinner, perhaps?'

She looked at him then. 'Oh—that would be nice, but I'm not sure——'

Uncle Oscar, who only feigned deafness when he didn't want to hear something, interrupted testily. 'Don't dither, miss, it's not often you get the chance to go out with someone like James. A distinguished medical man and much sought-after too. You go and make all the pretty girls spit with rage.'

Deborah said matter-of-factly, 'There's not much fear of that, but I'll let you know at breakfast on Monday morning.'

'Ha—going to stay out half the night, are you?' He looked crafty. 'Still holding hands, are you?'

She withdrew her hand from Sir James's clasp, who laughed easily and observed that Uncle Oscar was the most entertaining person he had ever had the good fortune to meet. He looked down at Deborah as he spoke and said with just the right amount of casual friendliness, 'I'll call for you about half-past six, if I may? There's a nice quiet hotel at Sutton Benger; you can tell me all your news over dinner.'

'I must ask Mrs Soames . . .'

'Of course, but I'll see her presently.'

She went back to the kitchen to get the cup and saucer and replenish the cold coffee-pot and the two men sat talking for half an hour before Sir James, saying that he still had to see Peter and get Bellum, got up to go. He shook the old man's hand and went to Deborah, sitting composedly in a chair, her hands tidily in her lap.

'We'll meet again tomorrow,' he said, and bent and kissed her cheek and let himself out into the garden in search of Peter Soames and Bellum.

Deborah got up and busied herself collecting cups and loading the tray, waiting for Uncle Oscar to bellow with laughter or bawl some jeering remark. The kiss had been unexpected and delightful but Uncle Oscar would take the magic from it with one of his rude remarks.

He said nothing, which surprised her, and she went off to the kitchen feeling relieved and at the same time amazed. She would have been even more surprised if she had seen his grin and heard his soft, 'Well, well—that I should live to see the day—always thought he was a confirmed bachelor, too.' He polished his glasses and when Deborah got back he was deep in his newspaper.

She dressed with great care on Sunday evening, pleased to see that the grey dress looked just as nice on her as it had when she had bought it. She fancied, erroneously, that its sober colour subdued the carroty hair to an acceptable auburn, and, as pleased with her person as her limited good looks allowed, she went downstairs, back to Uncle Oscar's room, to wait for Sir James.

That gentleman, she had no doubt, would have something nasty to say about her appearance and she was prepared for that. Only he wasn't nasty at all. 'Amazing what a decent dress does for a girl,' was all he said, a remark which she might take whichever way she chose.

She was on her hands and knees grovelling under a wall cabinet for Uncle Oscar's second pair of slippers which he had kicked there in a fit of pique, when Sir James came quickly into the room from the garden. He stood for a moment admiring the shapely portion of Deborah's person visible, before saying, 'Good evening—can I help?' in just the right kind of casual voice.

There was a gleam in his eye as he watched her wriggle out and stand up but when she looked at him his face bore a look of such blandness that she said matter-of-factly, 'It's all right, thank you—just Mr Trent's slippers.' Then she added as an afterthought, 'Hello.'

He smiled then. 'Hello, Deborah—I like the dress.'

Uncle Oscar, uncharacteristically silent, snorted, but as she wished him goodnight he grumbled, 'I suppose you'll be back at all hours...'

'You overlook the fact that I've reached the years of discretion and Deborah has to get up in the morning,' said Sir James equably, a remark which served to cast a shadow over Deborah's evening. The awful thought that he had asked her out from a sense of duty lay so heavy upon her that she added her assurance with a briskness which she repeated when they bade goodbye to the Soameses before going out to the car.

Sir James had perceived his mistake and correctly read the look on Deborah's face and laid himself out to smooth things over...something he did so well with undemanding small talk, aided by Bellum's obvious delight at the sight of her, that after a while she decided that she had been mistaken and began to enjoy her evening.

He had told her where they were going and it was only a short drive. The Bell House was a country hotel just outside Chippenham, set in a charming garden. Bellum, allowed to refresh himself for a few minutes, got back into the car behind the wheel and they went into its pleasant bar. Sir James had chosen well; the restaurant was charming; Deborah, warmed by sherry, surveyed it from their table set in a small alcove and noted with satisfaction that the other women there were dressed very much as she was. She gave a small sigh of relief and Sir James allowed himself a smile. 'I hope you are hungry—I've been gardening all day and I am ravenous.'

'Oh—you're staying somewhere near here?'

'Yes, not too far. It is a very pretty garden even now that summer is almost over. I'll take you to see it when we leave here.'

'It'll be dark.'

'There is a full moon and it can be lighted from the house.'

'They won't mind? The people you're staying with?'

'No.' He smiled and her heart turned over, an exciting sensation which she tried to suppress by studying the menu. 'Mushrooms in garlic with a cream sauce,' she said because she had to say something ordinary as quickly as possible. 'And then fish—sole *bonne femme* please.'

It wasn't until she was spooning up the last delicious mouthfuls of peach melba that he began to probe, very delicately, the plans for her future.

The Meursault 1989 Gauthay-Cadet had loosened her usually discreet tongue. Sir James topped up her glass and waited patiently.

'Well, I hope Mrs Soames will give me a good reference so that I can go to a really good agency and get another job quickly. Not in London, of course, because I might meet Walter or Barbara...'

'You don't wish to see them again?' His voice was very quiet.

'No, oh, no. They don't like me, you see; we never got on...' She stopped then, suddenly aware that she was letting her tongue run away with her. 'What a delightful place this is,' she said chattily.

'I'm glad you like it.' He began to tell her about the hotel and her suspicion that she had said too much about herself faded, just as he had meant it to.

As they got back into the car he suggested that they make a small detour. 'It is such a lovely evening and you can take a quick look at the garden I was telling you about.'

He drove north over the M4, going towards Malmesbury but turning off on to a country road after a mile or two. The moonlight was clear and very bright and the fields and trees were silvered by it. They passed through a small village, little more than a handful of cottages and a small church, and began to climb a gentle hill. The road turned at the top and dipped down towards another village, larger, with a narrow stream running alongside the road. They passed a small village green with the church at one side of it and a circle of cottages facing it and at the end of the narrow street turned in through tall brick pillars, to stop before a rambling half-timbered house with steep gables. The walls were whitewashed and the windows small and latticed.

Sir James got out and opened the door for her and then let Bellum out from the back of the car.

'It's beautiful,' said Deborah. 'Sixteenth century? I don't know much about architecture. You're sure your friends won't mind?' She looked across the small sweep to the lighted windows to one side of the door.

He took her arm and when she shivered said, 'Wait, there's a scarf in the car.' He fetched it and put it around her shoulders and went on easily, 'Perhaps I didn't make myself clear—not friends. I live here whenever I can get away from London. You're right,' he went on smoothly before she could say anything, 'it is very old—1550, to be exact. Edward VI gave it to my ancestor and it's been in the family ever since then. Mary Tudor would have confiscated it but it was even more rural than it is now and I imagine he lay low until Elizabeth came to the throne. He was a wily old man.'

He pushed open the door and Bellum tore down the wide hall, barking happily. The staircase swept gracefully up one wall, not as old as the house but blending its Georgian origins very nicely with the panelled walls, and at the end of the passage a wide old door was flung open to allow a very small plump woman to enter the hall. She was severely dressed, her hair, iron-grey, piled in a kind of whorl on top of her head. She had a round rosy face and twinkling brown eyes.

'There you are, Master James—and the young lady. There is a nice little fire in the drawing-room and a pot of coffee when you want it.'

'Thank you, Polly. Deborah, this is Polly, who looks after me here.' He smiled and Deborah offered her a hand and Polly said,

'Well, miss, it's a pleasure to meet you.'

'We're going to take a quick look at the garden,' said Sir James and swept Deborah down the hall, through the delightfully old-fashioned kitchen and out of the door beyond.

The sky was clear and the moon shone with a white radiance, even revealing flowerbeds and lawns, twisting paths and clumps of trees, arranged with careful haphazardness.

Very conscious of his hand tucked under her arm, Deborah asked, 'Was it always like this or have you made it?'

'A little of both. I haven't changed the plan of the garden at all, but of course I've planted a good deal. My father and his father planted more trees at the end of the lawn over there and I've put in a swimming-pool well out of sight.'

'Something smells lovely.'

'A gorgeous mixture, isn't it? There are still plenty of roses although we've had the best of the herbaceous border.'

'You must miss it . . .'

'Of course, but it's a quick run from London; I manage to spend most weekends here.'

They stopped walking for a moment to watch a hedgehog trot briskly across the path. 'There is a badger sett in the copse at the end of the garden. You like the country?'

They were going back towards the house, the lights from the windows streaming towards them. 'Yes.

When I was a little girl we lived at Nether Wallop but when Mother married again we moved to Hampstead.'

'You never went back?'

'No. My stepfather persuaded my mother to sell the house.' She hated talking about it and he was quick to realise that. He made a casual remark about the trio of Wallop villages and suggested a cup of coffee before he drove her back.

They went indoors then with Bellum trotting round them in circles down the hall and into a long low-ceilinged room, beamed and plastered, tapestry curtains covering the windows. The furniture was a mixture of oak, dark with age, and satinwood and applewood and, drawn up close to the fire, a Victorian table of burr walnut, supporting a silver tray on which stood a silver coffee-pot, simply chased and with a coat of arms engraved upon it. There was a matching cream jug and sugar bowl with it and two coffee-cups, the porcelain so thin that one could almost see through it. A small plate of wafer-thin biscuits completed the tray's contents and Deborah, offered a seat and asked to pour, said forthrightly, 'I'm afraid to touch anything. They're beautiful and old and I might drop something.'

'You have small neat hands,' observed Sir James placidly, 'and the things are in use every day when I am at home.'

A remark which gave her the courage to pour the coffee. He thought how nicely she did it.

The brass lantern clock struck the hour with a silvery tinkle and Deborah put down her cup and saucer. 'It's been a lovely evening,' she began, 'and thank you very much for taking me out. I think I'd better go back now.'

He agreed at once and she wondered if he had been a little bored with her company. His manners were far too good for her to be certain of that but she thought that she wasn't the kind of companion he would normally choose for an evening out. She got into the car with Bellum breathing great gusts of warm breath down her neck and reflected that never mind if he had been bored, it had been an evening to treasure.

The Soameses were still in their drawing-room. 'Had a pleasant evening?' asked Lottie. 'Uncle Oscar has gone to bed and I must say he has been a little trying. He said that you must go and say goodnight to him, Deborah, or he won't sleep.'

'I'm sorry, Mrs Soames, I won't go out again in the evening . . .' She stopped, blushing fiercely, for it had sounded as though she had expected that. 'I'll go and see him now on my way to bed. Goodnight.' She looked at Sir James lounging by the door. 'And thank you again for a delightful evening, Sir James.'

He sauntered towards her. 'It is I who was delighted, Deborah.' He opened the door and as she went past him brushed her cheek with a quick kiss.

Deborah fled across the hall, not looking back, and then crept into Uncle Oscar's sitting-room and over to the half-open door leading to his bedroom. His bedside light was still on and she paused in the doorway.

'Hah! So you're back, are you? Enjoyed yourself, I'll be bound. Did he kiss you goodnight?'

He glared at her over his spectacles and then took them off and looked away. 'Joking,' he mumbled, for he had seen her face.

'We had a lovely dinner,' she told him brightly, 'and then Sir James took me to his house—I didn't know he lived only a few miles away. The garden was lovely—there was a hedgehog and the roses smelled so sweet.' Her voice trailed away into silence and the old man said gruffly,

'Glad you had a good time. Now go to bed.'

'Yes, I will. Can I do anything for you before I go, Mr Trent?'

He heaved himself over in the half-tester bed. 'Nothing, I'm going to sleep.'

Deborah had been in bed for some time before she heard the Bentley's almost silent departure. That was that, she told herself firmly; the sooner she put the silly romantic ideas out of her head and bent her mind to her future, the better. The weeks were creeping by and she had made no plans for it. A few weeks—perhaps two months—and Uncle Oscar's daughter would be back ready to whisk him back to his home. It was a pity, thought Deborah sleepily, that she couldn't decide what was the best thing to do. She had prudently saved most of her wages but a training of any sort would take time and she didn't think she had enough to keep her for more than three or four months, even living as cheaply as possible. It would have to be a job where she earned as she learned. Teaching? She wasn't clever enough nor firm enough. Nursing? A roof over her head and her meals and just enough money to get by but she wasn't sure if she wanted to be a nurse. She liked looking after people but the more gruesome parts—theatre work, Casualty—she wouldn't be any good at all. Qualify as a nanny? But there again the fees at a reputable training college would be beyond her pocket. It left domestic work, a companion's post or a mother's help. She went to sleep on the thought and dreamed a dreadful muddle of missing trains, losing things and getting lost so that she woke in the small hours in a flurry of anxiety.

With the morning of course everything was reassuringly normal again. Uncle Oscar was in a pettish mood and she was kept occupied for the whole morning and at lunch Mrs Soames had a great deal to say about a big dinner dance she and her husband were to attend in a few weeks' time.

'Old friends,' she told Deborah, 'it's their eldest daughter's eighteenth birthday and there will be any number of people there. I wondered, Deborah, if you would mind making sure that the children are safely in their beds? I know they'll be looked after but if you could just cast an eye over them? We're bound to be back very late...'

'What about me?' demanded Uncle Oscar. 'Miss here is supposed to look after me.'

It took the rest of the meal and the promise of a game of chess to placate him.

The weeks slipped peacefully along in their accustomed routine. Summer was over and when Deborah went to Chippenham on her day off she laid out some of her money on a corduroy skirt in dark brown, a couple of shirt blouses and a honey-coloured wool sweater. It was a 'second' and therefore cheap but she thought it unlikely that anyone would notice the small flaw halfway up the back. She still had her suit and a pair of stout shoes and the grey dress should she need to dress up at any time—very unlikely, she told herself unless the Soameses had a dinner party and expected her to attend. So far, when they had had guests, Uncle Oscar had refused to join them and the pair of them had dined in his room. Probably a relief for everyone concerned.

On the day of the dinner dance Uncle Oscar decided to play up. He had a headache, he declared when Deborah went to wish him 'good morning'; he would breakfast in bed which meant that, in order to keep the peace in the kitchen, she had to lay a tray, load it with food and take it to him. To her offers of something for the headache she received the sharp observation that she could mind her own business, a remark which she ignored, merely pouring his coffee for him, making sure that his boiled egg was exactly as he liked it, and then taking herself off to the dining-room where she found the family already at breakfast.

Mrs Soames looked up as she sat down at the table. 'Good morning, Deborah. I could hear Uncle raging—what's really wrong?'

'I don't think it's anything to worry about; he said that he had a headache but he is eating his breakfast.'

'Oh, good. I've a letter here from his daughter; she doesn't say exactly when she will be back to collect him but very soon now.'

Deborah said steadily, 'I'm sure he will be very pleased to see her again—I think he must be very fond of her.'

'Oh, he is. We'll talk about it tomorrow, shall we? There'll be no time today. It's half an hour's drive this evening. We'll have to leave soon after seven o'clock; do you suppose that you can persuade Uncle Oscar to have dinner just a little bit later than usual so that you can see to the children?'

'I'll think of something,' said Deborah, surprised that her voice sounded quite normal. Her insides were trembling with the prospect of leaving although she reminded herself that she had known that it would happen. Anyway she would have to wait until tomorrow when Mrs Soames would have time to talk to her about it. She finished her breakfast with her usual calm and went back to Uncle Oscar, who was stomping around his sitting-room, demanding hot water and another pot of coffee.

'Is the headache better?' asked Deborah mildly.

'Headache, miss? I never have headaches.'

He was difficult all day; Deborah had no time to worry about her own concerns and by the time the Soameses were ready to leave that evening she was tired and rather cross. Uncle Oscar had tried her patience to its utmost limit and it was a great relief to leave him grumbling and growling to himself while she went upstairs to say goodnight to the children, which gave the housekeeper time to go to the kitchen and see about dinner, a meal which passed off with him in a slightly better frame of mind, so that after a few games of racing demon he retired to bed. Deborah took another look at the children and went to bed herself to lie wide awake and worry.

Mrs Soames, full of gossip about the evening's entertainment, had her coffee with her uncle and Deborah the next morning. It had been a marvellous evening, she told them, 'Crowds of people I had never met before, but so nice to see old friends and acquaintances again. An old school friend I haven't seen for years—just imagine meeting again after all this time. She had brought along some friends staying with her; we had such an interesting talk.'

Uncle Oscar dropped off to sleep after a time and Mrs Soames put down her coffee-cup, cast a look at him to make sure that he really was asleep and said, 'His daughter's coming back tomorrow—rather earlier than expected—I think we'd better tell him when he wakes up, don't you? Will you stay on for a day or two, Deborah, get his things packed up and so on? He's going to miss you.' She smiled her friendly smile. 'I dare say you've got a job to go to? Someone like you must be worth her weight in gold. Stay until the end of the week so that you have time to make any arrangements...'

Deborah thanked her. She liked Mrs Soames; warm-hearted and kind and quite unaware of how the other half lived. The end of the week would suit her very well, she told her.

Uncle Oscar, when told the news, expressed his pleasure in no uncertain terms at the same time wanting to know about Deborah.

'Where will you go?' he demanded to know.

'To another job,' she told him serenely so that he took it for granted that she had one waiting for her.

'I'll miss you,' he told her gruffly.

'I'll miss you, too.'

She spent the rest of the day sorting out his books and papers and all the odds and ends he found essential for his comfort, and on the following morning she got Edith to fetch his luggage and started to pack for him.

She was halfway through this task, on her knees before the bookcase sorting out what was to go and what was to be left, when Edith appeared at the door. 'Visitors for you, Miss Everett,' she said as she ushered in Barbara and Walter.

She got to her feet, speechless with shock, and it was Uncle Oscar, coming out of his bedroom with a pile of old magazines, who asked, 'Who are these people? Did I invite them?'

'I'm sorry, Mr Trent, they are people I know. Edith showed them in here. I expect she thought I was alone.'

'Well, you're not,' said the old man testily. 'What do they want?'

Walter advanced, hand outstretched. 'May I introduce myself and my sister? Walter and Barbara, Deborah's stepbrother and sister.'

Uncle Oscar ignored the hand. 'Well, what do you want?'

'Why, to see Deborah.' Walter was at his most pompous. 'We were at a party yesterday, you know, staying with old friends, great pals of Mrs Soames's it seems. She had a great deal to say about Deborah. We were wondering where she was. It couldn't be a better time.' He smiled around him. 'I heard that she is to leave within a day or so. She will of course, come home with us.'

'No,' said Deborah and added, 'And you can't make me.'

'You have no job to go to?' asked Walter and, before she could think up a suitable fib, he said, 'No, I see that you haven't—in that case there is no reason why you shouldn't come back home with us.'

'There is a good reason,' Sir James's quiet voice, and his firm hand grasping hers, sent Deborah's heart thudding. 'Deborah and I are going to be married.' He let go of her hand and flung a great arm around her shoulders. 'How very fortunate that I should get here in time to make that quite clear.'

CHAPTER SEVEN

UNCLE OSCAR might be old and crochety but there was nothing wrong with his wits.

'Ah, James, I was expecting you. Come to fetch Deborah, have you?' He studied Barbara and Walter with a cold eye. 'No need for you to be here, is there? Nice to have met you, good day. Edith will show you out.'

'I don't believe it,' Walter blustered. He caught Sir James's cold eye and added uncertainly, 'We've rather lost touch.'

Sir James took his arm from Deborah and went to the door. He didn't say anything at all as Barbara and Walter went past him and it was only when he had shut the door with a decisive snap behind them that she saw that he was very angry.

She said in a small voice. 'I'm sorry about that. I had no idea—I don't know how they discovered that I was here.'

'At the party, weren't they? Heard them say so.' Uncle Oscar was peering at her over his spectacles. 'Got news of you. Want you home, do they?'

Deborah shivered. 'I couldn't possibly...' She addressed Sir James's passive face. 'Thank you very much Sir James, it was most kind of you.' Despite her best efforts two tears trickled down her cheeks and she put up a hand and wiped them aside.

'Now, now, no tears.' Sir James was briskly firm and friendly. 'You shan't go with them if you don't want to. You're quite safe here.'

'No, she isn't—my daughter's coming today, Deborah's off somewhere or other. Tricky situation.'

'Easily solved. I'm here for lunch. Be ready to leave about two o'clock, will you?'

'Leave? But where am I going?'

'You'll stay in safe hands until you've fixed up another job. Don't argue, there's a good girl, just do as I say and trust me.'

She gave him a thoughtful look, the tears still trickling. She gave a small sniff. 'Of course I trust you. You didn't have to say that we were—were going to be married, you know.'

'It was the first thing that entered my head,' he told her carelessly. 'As long as they don't cross your path again, they'll not know anything different.'

'Well, thank you very much, I'm very grateful.'

She blew her small nose in a no-nonsense manner. 'I'll let Mrs Soames know you're here, shall I? She's downstairs with Mrs Hewish.'

She went to the door and with her hand on it paused. 'Do you suppose they've gone?'

'Ah—stupid of me. I'll have a look.' Sir James went past her, closing the door behind him, and Uncle Oscar said, 'A very reliable man, is James. You can trust him.'

Sir James came back this time with Bellum at his heels. 'Edith assures me that they have gone.' He held the door for her and she went past him into the hall. Edith was there.

She said in an apologetic voice, 'I'm sorry, miss—they said you were expecting them, and Mrs Soames being downstairs...'

'It's all right, Edith, it wasn't in the least your fault. They've gone.'

'Yes, miss. Staying with those friends of Mrs Soames's for the party last night.'

She went on downstairs and found Mrs Soames, happily unaware of the visitors but delighted that Sir James had arrived. 'In the drawing-room, is he?'

'With Mr Trent. Shall I ask him to go to the drawing-room?'

'No, no. I'll come and fetch him myself. We can all have coffee...'

It didn't seem quite the right time to tell Mrs Soames that she would be leaving that afternoon; anyway, Sir James, with his polished bedside manner, would deal with that.

He did too, with a calm good sense which made the whole thing seem ordinary and rather amusing. Mrs Soames, once she had learnt what had happened, was full of apologies. 'My tongue,' she said unhappily, 'I should have held it—gossiping like that.' She smiled apologetically at Deborah. 'I was boosting you to the skies, I suppose. I hadn't seen these friends for ages and of course they talked about you. I had no idea, Deborah...' Deborah murmured something. Everything was actually happening so fast that she hadn't caught up; of one thing she was certain, she had to know just where Sir James was taking her.

Lottie Soames beamed around her. 'I must say, that was some quick thinking on your part, James; what a good thing...' She caught his eye and almost without a pause went on, 'Deborah, if you are to leave us after lunch, you'll want to pack. I'm sorry you have to go like this but you don't want to meet those horrid people again, do you? We're all so sorry to see you go.'

Deborah went, pursued by grumbles from Uncle Oscar who was complaining that life would be dull without her. 'I shall come to the wedding,' he told Sir James in a belligerent voice.

'Of course you shall,' said Sir James promptly, and Mrs Soames said,

'You're joking, of course.' And then as an afterthought she asked. 'You're not thinking of getting married, James? After all this time...'

'The idea has crossed my mind.'

'Oh, good, and about time too. I suppose it's no good me asking anything else?'

'No good at all, Lottie.'

'How about a game of chess?' Uncle Oscar had got to his feet. 'It's hours to lunch.'

When Deborah went downstairs presently, her things packed, wearing the suit once more, she found the two men at their game. 'Go away, miss,' said Uncle Oscar. 'This is a serious game and I won't be distracted.'

She studied the chessboard. 'If you moved your pawn——'

'Oh, go away and wash your hair or whatever women do.' He put out a hand and caught hers. 'I shall miss you.'

'And I you, Mr Trent, but the world's a very small place and we're bound to meet again.'

'I'd forgotten. I'm definitely coming to dance at your wedding.'

'Oh, good, only wait until I find a husband, won't you?'

'Don't leave it too long, I'll not be around forever. Now go away, do—James has put me on the spot and I need to think.'

She had hoped that Sir James would have told her where he was taking her but he hadn't spoken. She went in search of Mrs Soames and found her with her feet up on one of the sofas.

'I'm still getting over the dance, I can't do without my sleep and it will be days before I'm fit for anything. Thank heaven my cousin's coming.

'I've phoned Peter; he's coming back for lunch— he'll give you a cheque.' She said anxiously, 'You don't feel that we're getting rid of you?'

'No, of course not, Mrs Soames. I know you asked me to stay for a day or two but there's really no need, is there? And I would like to get away as soon as possible. Walter is a very persistent man. I hope he won't come bothering you.'

'He'll get short shrift if he does,' said Mrs Soames cheerfully. 'Besides, he thinks you're going to marry James, and I don't suppose he knows who he is anyway! So he'll have lost all track of you.'

Deborah said, 'Yes,' doubtfully, wondering just where Sir James was taking her. Perhaps he knew of a job...

She had no chance to ask him; Mrs Soames's cousin arrived before lunch apparently once more ready and willing to look after her irascible parent and Deborah spent some time with her since Uncle Oscar, once he had greeted his daughter, told her to go away until the game of chess was finished. At lunch the conversation ranged over a vast number of topics and not one of them personal and afterwards Mr Soames took her off to his study to give her a reference and her cheque with a generous addition since she had been so splendid with Uncle Oscar and was having to leave rather sooner than they had intended. 'Don't know what Lottie would have done without you,' her employer told her in his friendly way. 'The old man's a handful and even though we're very fond of him it'll be a relief when he goes home in a couple of days' time. Got enough money, have you? I suppose James has a job in mind for you—that was a stroke of luck that he turned up just in time to get rid of your step-brother and sister.'

She agreed quietly. It had indeed been a stroke of luck, but where was it leading? The moment she was in the car she would find out.

As he drove away she waved to the little group standing on the porch and then settled back in her seat, Bellum as usual huffing and puffing gently into the back of her neck.

'Sir James...' she began and stopped because she wasn't sure how to go on. He obligingly helped her.

'I must admire your restraint, Deborah; you do so want to know where you are going, don't you?'

'Well, of course I do.' She sounded peevish, what with the morning's unpleasant excitement and the rush to pack and say goodbye.

'To my old nanny. I would have taken you to my mother but she's in Scotland with one of my sisters.'

'But she might not want to have me...'

'She will be delighted; she loves mothering people, animals, birds—anything living. You stay there for a day or two and get your breath and decide what you want to do.'

'Well, yes, thank you—I must find something.' She tried not to sound so worried.

'You will. There has hardly been time yet, has there?' he reminded her gently.

'No. I'm being silly—sorry—only everything happened rather quickly and—I hadn't expected to see Walter and Barbara.'

'You're afraid of them?' His voice was very kind.

'Yes, a little—Walter—they don't like to be thwarted, you see.'

'I didn't take to him,' said Sir James in a dry voice. 'I think that you will be safe enough with Nanny and when you get a job allow me to check thoroughly before you accept it.'

'You're awfully kind.'

'I would do the same thing for my sisters or friends.'

A remark which she felt rather put her in her place. All the same she persevered, 'Where does she live, your nanny?'

'East Garston—north of Hungerford. We can use the motorway for almost the whole trip. She expects us for tea.'

She looked at him and he added, 'I phoned her while you were packing.'

She sat quietly then, turning over in her mind what was best to be done. She was a bit hazy as to where East Garston was but if it was near Hungerford then Swindon and Henley-on-Thames, even Reading, weren't too far away, and surely there would be work of some kind in one of them. It would have to be a job as mother's help for no one would expect training for such work, although heaven knew she had had enough of that. Several months, perhaps a year, in such a job and she could save money and then train for something. Perhaps nursing was the answer after all but she hesitated to ask Sir James about that; he might think that she expected him to help her even more than he had already done.

It wasn't a great distance and twelve miles or so after he had by-passed Swindon Sir James turned off on to a side-road and then slowed the car into a narrow country road, going slowly downhill. The village looked delightful: a nice mixture of thatch and red tiles as they entered its main street, and lining the road to the grey Norman church were whitewashed cottages each with its own small bridge over the little stream running before their doors. He stopped before the last cottage in the row and got out to open Deborah's door and release Bellum, who pranced across the bridge to bark happily at the person standing at the open door.

Deborah had been worrying about Nanny; she might dislike her on sight. Nannies were known to be decisive people with sharp tongues and she had been foisted on her at a moment's notice. She need not have worried, however; Sir James hugged the stout little person, kissed her cheek and said, 'Well, Trotty, here is Deborah. I know you'll look after her.'

Deborah put out a hand and had it shaken while elderly blue eyes studied her face. 'That I will, love. Come in, tea's ready and Mr James, just you keep that Bellum of yours nice and quiet—my Maudie has just had four of the sweetest kittens. They're in the kitchen by the stove.'

She had ushered them into a small room, rather full of furniture, with photos in a variety of frames arranged wherever there was a space. A small round table had been covered by a white cloth with a crocheted edge, and plates and cups and saucers laid upon it. There was a plate of thin bread and butter, a sponge cake and a substantial fruit cake on a glass stand. 'Made the cake this morning,' said Nanny, 'but you'll eat your bread and butter first.' She bustled away to make the tea and then came back again. 'I dare say Deborah would like to wash her hands,' she said and Deborah obediently got up and went up the narrow winding staircase. The landing was just large enough to turn round in and there were three doors. Nanny opened one of these. 'There you are, love. The towels on the rail are yours. Your room is here.' She opened another door. 'But you can settle in once Mr James has gone. I'll fetch that tea...'

She trotted away and when Deborah went downstairs she found the sitting-room empty. 'We're in the kitchen,' said Sir James. 'Come in here and see Maudie's family.'

The little cat was a tabby with a great deal of white on her chest and paws and the kittens were a mixture of ginger, black and tabby. They all ignored their visitors; even Bellum, sniffing cautiously over the rim of the basket, was ignored. 'Nice, eh?' said Nanny. 'You shall have one, Mr James, once they are old enough to leave their Ma.'

'Thank you, Trotty; Tibbles will doubtless take it under her wing.' He glanced at Deborah. 'Tibbles is my housekeeper's cat—not at the cottage—in London.'

They had a splendid tea and presently Sir James got up to go. He kissed Trotty's plump cheek, assured Deborah that he would see her again at some time, and, with a friendly nod, whistled to Bellum and went back over the bridge to his car, got in and drove away with a careless wave.

She had been left, reflected Deborah indignantly, like a parcel at the post office. The sooner she got work and went away the better. Loving a man who treated you like an object of charity was very wearing. It was a great pity that despite that she loved him still.

'Now up you go and put away your things,' said Nanny, and when Deborah said meekly, 'Yes, Miss Trott,' she said,

'You have no call to say that, dearie, everyone calls me Trotty, so I hope you'll do the same. It'll be a great treat to have company. I like a bit of a gossip.'

Deborah unpacked in the little room with its small white bed and coloured counterpane and flowered curtains at the window. There was a cupboard in one wall and a chest of drawers as well as a small dressing-table.

She went downstairs and found Trotty in the kitchen, frying sausages. When she said how pretty her room was, Trotty said, 'Well, love, the children come here off and on.' She didn't volunteer any more information and Deborah didn't like to ask and presently they sat down to their supper while Trotty gave her all the news of the village. 'You'll get to know them soon enough,' she told Deborah, 'they're very friendly folk.'

'Well, I should think I wouldn't be here long enough for that. I thought I'd go into Hungerford tomorrow if you don't mind and see about finding a job.'

'You take my advice and wait a day or two, love. Sir James wouldn't like that at all. Told me you was to rest up for a day or two—had a nasty shock, he said. You'd do better to spy out the land a bit.

Trained, are you?' and when Deborah shook her head. 'Then you'd do better in Reading or Henley.'

They washed up the supper things together and had a cup of tea before Deborah was sent to bed in the kindest possible manner. 'Breakfast at eight o'clock, love—and have your bath tonight—there's plenty of hot water.'

There was sense in Trotty's advice. Deborah spent the next two days looking at bus timetables, deciding on which town she would try first. She would need to go to the bank anyway; she had a cheque to pay in and she needed to know just how much money she had and then withdraw some of it. There would be bus fares and meals and fees at the agencies. She had also to buy a raincoat before the wet weather came.

She went down to breakfast on the third day and told Trotty that she would like to go into Newbury. It had been a town she had overlooked but there was a bus service and it wasn't too far, yet large enough to have her bank and possibly some kind of an agency.

'Bus goes in half an hour,' said Trotty briskly. 'You go, love, and look round. There's a nice little café in the High Street but you come back in good time for your tea, mind.'

Newbury was larger than she had expected; she had a cup of coffee, took a quick look at the shops, found her bank and then began to search for an agency. She found one down a small side-street and since it looked prosperous and well kept, she went inside.

Going back into the street presently, she marvelled at her good luck. There were three jobs which were suitable—all of them for a mother's help and all of them in Newbury. She had been advised to write and apply to all of them before going for interviews. She had had to pay a fee, of course, and if she took one of the jobs offered she would have to pay a percentage of her first week's pay too. Not an impulsive girl, she was carried away with her good fortune and bought paper and envelopes and found a post office where she wrote her letters at one of the side-counters and posted them there and then. This done, she found the café Trotty had recommended and had a rather extravagant meal, and then had another look at the shops and a sharp-eyed tour of Marks and Spencer. She would need one or two things if she got a job...

She told Trotty all about it when she got back and Trotty listened without interruption and when she had finished said, 'Mr James said he'd look 'em over, didn't he? You'd better wait and see what he says.'

Deborah agreed reluctantly. 'If I don't hear from him in a few days, though, I think I'd better at least go for interviews if they want them. I might be missing a good job. I'm sure Sir James is a very busy man and must have a great many other things to think about.'

'He'll telephone, I have no doubt,' said Trotty.

Deborah received replies to each of her letters, all of them asking her to go for an interview, and there had been no word from Sir James. Trotty waited until Deborah had gone to the village shop and then telephoned his house in London. Dobbs, as mournful as ever, told her that he had been called away to foreign parts. 'Some high and mighty had a stroke or something,' he explained. 'No telling when he'll be back.'

Trotty didn't tell Deborah that she had telephoned but she read the three letters carefully and reluctantly and agreed that she should at least go and see what kind of jobs they were. So Deborah made appointments for all three and took the bus to Newbury again.

The first one was no good; the lady of the house wanted a strong girl capable of lifting her obese mother in and out of bed, feeding her and getting her in and out of the bath. They agreed mutually that Deborah wasn't suitable. The second was more hopeful until it was disclosed that one of the four children in the family was an epileptic and that Deborah would be responsible for her both day and night. At the third house things seemed more than suitable. She was shown her room; small but very clean and neat and she would have reasonable free time. There would be a certain amount of housework, of course, and there were three schoolchildren but there was a daily cleaner too. The house was in a pleasant part of the town and the wages were adequate although not over-generous. Deborah agreed to start working in two days' time and, on the strength of security in the foreseeable future, went to Marks and Spencer and bought herself a raincoat.

She went back to Trotty feeling that at least she had made a start. The niggling thought that Sir James had said that he wanted to know of any job she might want to take bothered her a little but it was some time now since he had gone and she had to have work as soon as possible.

When Deborah had gone to bed Trotty took it upon herself to telephone Sir James again. Dobbs answered. No word of Sir James—he sounded more depressed than ever—but then, he pointed out, he very seldom let his household know when he would return; he would just turn up some day, back from a remote part of the world.

'Well, let me know when he does get back,' said Miss Trott. 'It's urgent.'

Deborah hated leaving the dear little cottage and her kind hostess. Trotty had refused to let her contribute to her keep so she had gone into Hungerford and bought an early morning tea set. She didn't think that Trotty would use it but she might if she had a guest and she seemed delighted with it.

Deborah had no chance to repine. Mrs Woods was pleasant enough, the children much like any other children—she had met them when she had gone for her interview and they were quite prepared to accept her as a member of the household—but after the first day or two she was expected to do rather more than she had been told; the daily cleaner was by no means reliable and on the days when she chose not to turn up Deborah had her hands more than full. Moreover, Mrs Woods had frequent attacks of migraine. Nevertheless, she was determined to make the best of it and when she wrote to Trotty she took care to paint a cheerful picture of her life. She was lonely after the old lady's bracing company and she missed Maudie and the kittens and above all she minded very much that Sir James hadn't kept his promise. He was a busy man, she understood that, and he must have dozens of friends and it was easy to forget her. It was a pity, she reflected sadly, that she couldn't forget him.

He hadn't forgotten her but, caught up on the other side of the world doing his best to keep alive a man for whom it was important to stay that way, he had tucked her into the back of his mind while his skilled brain coped with the situation. It was a remote part of the globe and even if he could have telephoned or sent a cable he had no hope of following them up at the moment. He was a man of patience and self-control and for the moment there was nothing to be done about it.

Deborah had been with Mrs Woods just over a week when the eldest child became ill, coughing and sneezing and with streaming eyes. It wasn't long before a rash appeared on the child's forehead and he was put to bed.

'Measles,' said Mrs Woods, 'and I suppose the other two will catch it!'

Which they did on the same day that Mrs Woods declared that she would have to stay in her room with a migraine and the daily cleaner, announcing that she wasn't going to work where there was illness, walked out of the house.

The children were feverish and ill and Deborah was forced to tiptoe into Mrs Woods's room and ask if she could get the doctor.

'It's only measles,' said Mrs Woods, 'but I suppose he had better come.'

He was a pleasant man, overworked and tired, but he examined the children, pronounced them to be feverish, advised that their rooms be darkened and said that he could come again if Deborah was worried.

There was no time to be worried; Mr Woods was a traveller in insurance and away for days at a time, Mrs Woods declared herself unable to lift her head from the pillow; Deborah ploughed her way through the next few days, glad to find that the children rapidly improved and that Mrs Woods was able to face some of the easier chores around the house. At least, now that she was feeling better, Deborah was able to go to the shops and buy their food. It was almost a week later when Deborah, after a restless night, got up with all the symptoms of a heavy cold, took a look in the mirror and saw the red blotches on her forehead.

It was awkward to say the least. She dressed, hoping that she would feel better as the day wore on, but the rash, by the time she was ready to go downstairs, was spreading rapidly. There was nothing for it but to go and tell Mrs Woods.

That lady received the news coldly. 'Who is to look after the children?' she wanted to know. 'I feel my migraine coming on and I simply cannot cope. You will have to do the best you can while I think of something. After all, it is only measles.'

Deborah wasn't listening; she felt ill and keeping on her feet was becoming more and more hazardous, besides she felt very cold... With a whispered apology she fell in a tidy heap on to Mrs Woods's bedroom carpet.

Sir James, returning at last to his house in London, was met in the hall by Dobbs, looking more solemn than ever. Sir James, exchanging civilities with him, asked briskly if there was any news. 'Good or bad,' he added, 'for you look remarkably down in the mouth.'

'Well, I am, so to speak,' said Dobbs. 'There's Nanny Trott telephoning me something frantic—wants to speak to you the minute you get back and me not having the least idea when that would be since, begging your pardon, Sir James, you never let fall so much as a hint...'

Sir James had divested himself of his coat and his case; now he said sharply. 'When did Trotty first telephone, Dobbs?'

'Quite a while ago,' said his devoted servant with irritating vagueness. 'Something to do with the young lady leaving for a job, but the last few days she's phoned very often, every day at least—sometimes twice.'

Sir James crossed to his study, received Bellum's delighted welcome in an absentminded manner and picked up the phone. 'What's wrong, Trotty?'

Miss Trott wasted no time in polite enquiries concerning his trip.

'Deborah—she's written to me faithful-like twice a week and I've heard nothing for four days and it's not like her; besides I've got one of my feelings.'

'Where is she, Trotty?' He sounded so matter-of-fact that she calmed down a little. 'That's just it—she waited to hear from you and there was this job in Newbury; she thought you'd forgotten her, very sure of that she was, said the job was too good to miss, went almost two weeks ago and promised to write at least twice a week and drat me I've mislaid the woman's name so I can't telephone.'

'You have her address?'

'Yes, I've kept her letters.'

Sir James glanced at his watch. He had returned on an overnight flight, a long one, and he was tired and hungry and there was work waiting for him.

'There are one or two things I must see to, Trotty, but I'll be with you some time this afternoon. Don't worry—the letter might have gone astray or Deborah may have forgotten to write.'

He hung up and went away to shower and shave and change and presently went downstairs to find Dobbs in the hall. 'You'll have your breakfast, sir—body and soul must be kept together. I've put your letters by the table so that you can do two things at once.'

Sir James laid a hand on Dobb's shoulder. 'What would I do without you, Dobbs? Tell Mrs Dobbs I'm famished.'

He worked while he ate, by the time he had finished he had dealt with his post, telephoned his registrar, his receptionist, several of his colleagues at the hospital, and planned the week ahead. That done, he asked Dobbs to pack him a bag once more, got into his car, this time with Bellum for company, and drove himself down to Trotty's little cottage.

Trotty said ruefully, 'I shouldn't have let her go, but how was I to stop her, determined as she was . . .?'

'Don't blame yourself, Trotty. It's my fault, I had an urgent call to attend a patient in one of the more inaccessible parts of the world, and I had no idea that I would have to remain there with him for so long. Now, let me have the address and I'll go and see what Deborah is up to.'

'She's such a dear girl—don't you be angry with her, Mr James.' Miss Trott sounded just like a nanny. 'You like her, don't you?'

He smiled at her. 'Oh, yes, Trotty, I do. We'll be back presently.'

He left Bellum in the car and knocked on Mrs Woods's door and when Mrs Woods opened it said, 'Good afternoon. I understand that Miss Deborah Everett works for you. I wonder if I might see her?'

Mrs Woods eyed him with hard eyes. 'Works for me? That's a laugh. Caught the kids' measles and lying there in bed and me with my migraine and the daily woman not coming . . . who are you, anyway?'

'James Marlow. I am a doctor and an old family friend of Miss Everett's. I heard that she was working here and came to see her. I had no idea that she was ill.'

'Only been here a couple of weeks. Suited us very well but of course I can't have her ill in bed; she'll have to go.'

'Of course, Mrs . . .?' He paused with an enquiring smile. 'Woods? If possible I can take her back to her friend's house and relieve you of the responsibility.'

'Well, you'd better come in. You are a doctor, aren't you, and you do know Deborah?'

'Indeed I am and I do.'

She led the way upstairs. 'Terribly sorry the place is a bit untidy—all three children have had the measles and of course my migraine . . .'

He could hear the children; they sounded as though they were quarrelling and Mrs Woods paused on the stairs. 'My husband is away—he's a salesman; he has no idea. I wasn't brought up to this kind of life, Doctor.'

She opened one of the doors on the landing and he followed her in. Deborah lay in bed, her colourful hair in an untidy unbrushed tangle all over the pillow. Her eyes were puffy, her face too, and the measles had spread themselves lavishly in all directions. She looked very plain and not very clean, but over and above that she looked ill.

Sir James stood and looked at her from the foot of the bed and thought that she was the most beautiful girl in the world and at the same time gave way to self-mockery at such a ridiculous idea. Not that he allowed his thoughts to show. 'Miss Everett appears to be ill. You have had the doctor?'

Mrs Woods looked guilty. 'Well, I had thought I'd get him to come today. He came to see the children, but it's only measles—look how quickly they're getting over it.'

He didn't reply and Deborah coughed painfully and opened her eyes. She said in a husky voice. 'Better late than never.' She frowned. 'You forgot but it's quite all right. Please go away, I'm not feeling very well.'

He picked up a hot hand. 'I've come to take you to Trotty,' he told her.

'I won't go—all that extra work for her.' She coughed again.

Sir James spoke crisply. 'You cannot stay here, Mrs Woods has more than enough to do without nursing you, Deborah.'

She opened her eyes again. 'Oh, I'm sorry I'm such a nuisance. I could go to hospital.' She spoke in a peevish mutter.

'Leave everything to me,' said Sir James at his most soothing, and, since her head ached and she was tired, she closed her eyes at once and fell into a fitful sleep.

She was aware during the next half-hour or so of being disturbed but she was too weary to wake up.

CHAPTER EIGHT

WHEN Deborah did at last rouse herself she woke to see that she was back in her pretty little room at Trotty's cottage. Trotty was on one side of the bed and Sir James on the other. They were both looking at her, one with the brisk regard of a dyed-in-the-wool nanny intent on restoring her charge to a state of cleanliness and comfort, the other with a look of resigned tenderness. It was no good, reflected Sir James, Deborah had come into his life and wasn't going to go again.

He had a perfect bedside manner; he assumed it now. 'You are back with Trotty,' he told her in a comforting, firm voice. 'She is going to make you comfortable and then I shall examine you. You have had quite a bad dose of measles.'

Deborah's wits were still woolly; she was searching for a polite answer as he left the room. Somehow that upset her and she began to weep, the tears pouring down her grubby cheeks. Trotty said comfortingly, 'Now, now, everything's all right now, dearie. Just you let old Trotty give you a nice wash and a clean nightie.' She gave Deborah's measly person a hug and went to fetch a basin.

Half an hour later Deborah was lying back against her pillows. Her hair had lost a lot of its glory but at least it was brushed and plaited tidily and she was clean once more and in one of her fresh cotton nighties. She wished weakly that she had something prettier to put on but that didn't really matter—all the silk and lace in the world wouldn't disguise the blotchy rash.

Trotty had been quick and truly gentle but Deborah was tired out now. She very soon closed her eyes, content to be clean and comfortable; she would take a nap.

Then Sir James came back, dwarfing everything in the room with his vast size. He said in an impersonal voice, 'That's better. I'm going to examine you, Deborah. You have a nasty cough and I want to make sure that it's no worse than that.'

She opened one eye. 'Oh—yes, of course. I feel much better, thank you.'

He ignored this useless remark and Trotty turned back the bedclothes with a crisp, 'Now you just do what Sir James tells you, love.'

So Deborah breathed in and out, coughed and said 'One-one-one' when he told her to and stuck out her tongue and had her eyes examined and her ears peered into. The thought crossed her mind that he probably was paid a large fee for doing just that to his patients. She asked him, suddenly wishing to know, 'Do you get many patients with measles?'

Sir James, who hadn't seen a Koplik's spot for many years, assured her gravely that he didn't.

She would feel much better in a day or so, he told her in a low, kind voice. All she had to do was to stay quietly in bed, take the pills he prescribed for her and eat and drink what Trotty offered her.

'Are you going away again?'

He sat carefully on the side of the bed. 'Yes, but I shall return to see how you are getting on.'

'I'll be all right, really I will. You don't need to bother. I expect you're very busy.' She stopped to cough.

'Yes. Deborah, you are to do as I say, is that understood? You have a chest infection as well as measles. That will soon clear with the antibiotics but I must insist that you do as Trotty tells you.'

She nodded and held out a hand, to have it clasped in his firm grasp.

'I promise.'

'Good. Now go to sleep.'

So she did and when she woke, much refreshed, it was to learn from Trotty that Sir James had gone back to London. 'Got to catch up on his work,' said Trotty chattily, proffering pills and home-made lemonade. 'Him being away for all that time, it piled up.'

'Was he on holiday?' asked Deborah in her tired little voice.

'Lord bless you, no, love. Been thousands of miles away being consulted by some VIP, and not one of those places where you can just go and come back if you see what I mean. Now you go to sleep again and presently I shall bring up your supper and you'll have every scrap or my name's not Trott.'

It took several days before Deborah began to feel better; ample time in which to think about Sir James. Each morning when she woke she hoped that he might come, only to tell herself that he was a busy man with a life of his own and there was no need for him to visit her. He could have telephoned, she thought tiredly, but then why should he?

He telephoned each evening, long after she was asleep, and received a painstaking report from Trotty, and one night, quite late, he came. He trod soft-footed up the narrow stairs and stood by her bed, looking down at her. How small she looked and still rather fragile, but the rash was fading and her hair was beginning to glow once more. She looked very young, carroty lashes lying on her cheeks, her mouth slightly open. He bent and kissed her very gently and went downstairs to Trotty's coffee and sandwiches.

'You ought to be in your bed,' said Trotty gruffly.

'Driving is very restful, my dear, and I have no patients until midday tomorrow.' He studied her nice elderly face. 'You're not getting tired? Say the word and I'll have help here within a couple of hours.'

'Since when have I needed help, Mr James? Thank you all the same. The child's no trouble—as good as gold and does just what she's told to do. She's unhappy, though.' Trotty poured more coffee. 'What's to become of her?'

She peered at him over her spectacles when he didn't give an answer and then nodded her head. 'Well, well—that I should live to see the day...'

Sir James gave Bellum the last of his sandwich and got up to go.

'Take good care of her, Trotty.' He gave his old nanny a hug. 'And look after yourself. I have to go to Edinburgh for a couple of days but I'll be back as soon as I can. If you want me, get hold of Dobbs— he will know where I am.'

'Am I to tell Deborah that you came tonight?'

'No, don't do that, my dear.' He whistled to Bellum who had gone to look for more sandwiches and then got into his car and drove away.

As he drove he considered the future; he was deeply in love with Deborah, but he wasn't sure if she loved him. It seemed to him, a man of no conceit, that any feelings she might have for him would be born of gratitude and to take advantage of that was entirely against his principles. Now, what was to be done with her? Yet another job? Somewhere where he could see her regularly? Persuade her to stay with Trotty? He thought it unlikely that she would accept charity for a moment longer than she had to. Should he let her go? Let her find another job so that she would feel free to live her own life, make new friends, perhaps meet some younger man. It seemed to be the right answer. He would go and see her again, of course, for until she was quite well she was in his care, but once she was on her feet and fit again he would take care to distance himself from her; leave her to find her own feet. Only he would have to know where she was so that should she need help he could be there.

Deborah, unaware that her future was being planned for her in a manner which wouldn't have pleased her at all if she had known about it, rapidly improved. The rash went, colour came back into her cheeks and her hair, washed and shining once more, glowed with good health. She would have been perfectly happy if only she could have seen Sir James now and then, but it was another week before he arrived early one morning. He was on the way to his cottage, he explained to them, and thought he would call in and see how she was getting on.

'I'm quite well again,' she told him, 'and I'd like to start looking for another job.'

His ready agreement to this sent her heart into her shoes; he wanted to be rid of her and she couldn't blame him but all the same the prospect of a future without him, even infrequent glimpses of him, was hardly to be borne.

'Have you any ideas?' he asked her. 'Some sort of training—mother's helps are all very well, but they aren't of much help if you are a career girl at heart.'

Deborah, who had had no idea that he thought of her as anything so high-powered, none the less agreed because it seemed to her that he expected it.

She said with tremendous enthusiasm, 'Shorthand and typing and something called word processing—I thought I'd take a course; I've some money saved.'

'Splendid. Where do you intend to go?'

Since she had only just thought of it, she had no idea but she said briskly, 'Oh, London, I think—if I work hard I can get a job straight away.'

Sir James had his doubts. Somehow she didn't seem the right kind of person to sit at a desk all day; he wasn't even sure if she would ever master the skills she spoke of so airily. However, she had to have her chance of seeing more of life. He observed blandly that she seemed to have her future very well organised and there was no reason why she shouldn't make a success of it. A remark to which Deborah responded with just the right amount of enthusiasm while her heart, never far from her shoes, sank once more to their very soles.

They all had coffee together and, now that her future was so satisfactorily planned, it wasn't mentioned again. He bade her goodbye with a casual pleasantness which cut her to the heart and puzzled Trotty. Sir James had always been a deep one, she reflected, even as a small boy, and why he didn't just pick up the girl and run off with her and marry her was beyond her.

When he had gone she said, 'You're sure that's what you want to do, love? London's a great lonely place and where will you live?'

'Well, I'll find a room near the place I take the course—there are several advertised, you know, and if I work hard I should be able to get a good job within a few months.'

'Well you know best,' conceded Trotty, not believing it, 'but you're to let me know where you are, love, and promise me that if you're unhappy or short of money you'll tell me at once.'

'Of course I will,' promised Deborah, her fingers crossed behind her back. She had a strong affection for Trotty but she had every intention of disappearing once she had left the little cottage. Sir James expected her to make a new life for herself; after all, he had called her a career girl, a rather glamorous type, she had always thought, wearing beautifully cut suits and Italian shoes and with hair which shone like gold lacquer. She had no money for suits or shoes and nothing on earth would turn her carroty hair into gold lacquer, but there was no reason why, given reasonable luck, she couldn't work her way up and become frightfully successful. She was aware that this was nonsense even as she thought it, but she had to buoy up her flagging spirits.

Now she would have to put her words into actions; she answered several advertisements for commercial schools and spent time comparing them. Most of them held out promise of speedy perfection and high salaries but the only one which she could afford made no reference to these, merely stated that once the course was finished she might expect to find work as a shorthand typist. Fees were payable a month in advance and included the use of typewriters and word processors and, for those who wished, a further course in the use of the computer could be arranged.

There was just enough money to pay for a three-month course, although it was suggested that a further three months was advisable, and provided that she could find a room at a reasonable rent she felt reasonably confident that she could afford it. She would have to leave after the first three months, of course, but if she could type by then and have at least some idea of shorthand she could try for a job.

The question of a room was difficult. It didn't make sense to go to London and spend a day looking for lodgings but nor on the other hand did she relish the idea of arriving in town with no prospect of a bed ... It was Trotty who came to her aid. A friend, whom she hadn't seen for a couple of years but to whom she still wrote, had been recently widowed. She lived, most fortunately, a bus ride away from the commercial school where Deborah was enrolled, and Trotty was sure that she would be glad to rent a room to Deborah.

'She's a nice enough woman, mind you,' said Trotty, 'but from what I gather from her letters she's let herself go—spends a lot of time at bingo and watching TV. You could start off there, though, and have a look round.'

She wasn't at all happy about Deborah going to London; she had been so sure that Sir James had fallen in love at last and that he and Deborah would marry but now it seemed as though she had been mistaken. They couldn't have quarrelled, for they were never alone together; indeed he hadn't been near the cottage for ten days or more. The doubt that some glamorous creature had caught his attention in London became almost a certainty despite the fact that she found it hard to believe.

She did the best she could, though, and when Deborah was ready to leave saw that she had a covered basket with the wholesome food she felt sure was unobtainable in London. The basket was awkward to carry but Deborah thanked her and hugged her and promised to write in a cheerful voice which successfully hid her panic.

Sitting in the train, she had never felt so lonely. She would have felt less so if she could have heard Trotty on the phone to Sir James, giving every last detail of her departure, explaining about the room rented from an old friend and the rosy prospects of an office job in a few months' time. If Trotty had hoped for some inkling of his feelings, Sir James had no intention of revealing them. He thanked her for the information, expressed the hope that Deborah would make a good start in her new career, and rang off.

The address Miss Trott had given him was in the vicinity of London Bridge and he withstood a strong temptation to go and look at it. It wasn't a neighbourhood he would have chosen to live in and the idea of Deborah being there, away from the country and the fresh air, rankled. He had made the decision to keep away from her and give her a chance to do something with her life so he ignored the promptings of his heart and applied himself to his work, and when he received an urgent request to attend the bedside of an elderly patient holidaying on one of the more remote Greek islands, he accepted it. Trotty, when he phoned her, was upset, but she was too wise to say so; she said merely that she hoped he wouldn't be away too long and waited for him to ask about Deborah. Which he did in a casual manner which didn't deceive her in the least.

'I had a long letter from her; she seems to have settled down very nicely, says it's hard work but seems to like it.'

'Splendid,' said Sir James in a bland voice which gave nothing away.

Deborah's letters to Trotty were cheerful, chatty and presented a picture to the reader of a contented life which, while not completely untrue, was certainly not an accurate picture. The comfortable room she described with such detail was in fact a back bedroom in Trotty's friend's house, one in a terrace of rather downtrodden houses, grimed by pollution from the nearby railway station. It looked on to a small stretch of back garden, untended and littered with stray bits of rubbish and dirty papers, and the comfort of the room left much to be desired. True, the bed was comfortable enough, but the dressing-table, minus a castor, was wedged against a wall, a wad of newspaper under one leg, and the wardrobe door had a tendency to fly open for no reason at all. The room

was clean, though, and the bedlinen clean too, and
Deborah had the use of the front room downstairs if
she so wished. Mrs Squires was a friendly soul, no
longer even middle-aged, so she might be excused
from doing more than keeping the house tidy, something which she did only occasionally. She was ex-
tremely good-natured and full of good intentions and
liked to chat about her friend Miss Trott. It surprised
Deborah that they had been friends for two people
more unlike each other she had yet to meet.

Mrs Squires was a late riser so Deborah got up early
and arranged her own breakfast before taking the bus
to her classes. She went with the other students to a
nearby café for a roll and butter and a pot of tea at
midday and in the evening Mrs Squires cooked for
them both. She had been, she told Deborah, a good
cook in her day but now she tended to open tins and
defrost fast food, but Deborah, tired after her day's
studies, would have eaten anything put before her and
was grateful for a hot meal.

Life after the tranquillity of Trotty's cottage seemed
dull and monotonous but she had chosen it, determined to work hard and eventually get a worthwhile
job. All the same she was lonely, for although the
other students were friendly enough they treated her
with good-natured tolerance for she worked hard and
since she had no money to spare, never joined them
on their evening jaunts to the local pubs or cinema.
So her evenings were spent practising her shorthand,
a skill she doubted she would ever master, and helping
Mrs Squires clear away their supper and wash up. She
had been there for only a few days when she discovered Mrs Squires' cat, a thin, neglected beast who

slunk into the kitchen in search of food. Mrs Squires shooed it out, not unkindly but with no wish to be bothered with it. 'Cats can look after themselves,' she told Deborah. 'He was a pretty little kitten too, but he's a nuisance now. I'll have to get rid of him.'

'Would you mind if I had him?' asked Deborah. 'I'll pay for his food and look after him and he'll be company for me while I'm studying in the evenings in my room.'

'Well, I don't know—I suppose so. Why not? Just so long as he doesn't get under my feet.'

'Has he a name?'

'Buster. But he doesn't answer to it any more.'

Deborah looked at the grubby little beast, waiting so patiently for any scraps, and wondered when anyone had last called him by name, let alone spoken to him. She went out presently to the little corner shop run by a Pakistani family and open at all hours, and bought cat food and tinned milk and a packet of little crunchy biscuits she was assured all cats loved and bore them back to Mrs Squires' house. That lady had gone out to her bingo session so that Deborah was free to feed Buster and, while he was gobbling his supper, hunted for an old cardboard box. She lined it with old newspapers for lack of anything else and took it up to her room and rather to her surprise Buster went with her, circled the room cautiously and got into the box, where he sat giving himself a long-needed wash while she explored the possibilities of the window. It had a sill almost overhanging the narrow strip of roof over the back door; there was no reason why he shouldn't go in and out without Mrs Squires being bothered. She left the window wide open and sat down at the little card table by it and started on her shorthand. Presently Buster began to purr, a raucous sound, but then he was sadly out of practice, for he had had nothing to purr about, but it was a homely sound and Deborah paused to tell him so.

Mrs Squires would be late home and she went downstairs to make herself a cup of tea and leave everything ready for her breakfast in the morning. Buster went with her and she let him out into the back garden while she drank her tea and washed a cup. He didn't come in when she called and after a while she locked the door and went back to her room to get ready for bed, with the intention of going to the back door again at the last moment—something which wasn't necessary for there he was, sitting on the sill, washing his whiskers, very much at home.

'Clever boy,' said Deborah and offered him a snack meal before bedtime. She got into bed presently with the window opened just wide enough for him to creep in and out should he so wish but she need not have bothered for no sooner was she settled in bed than he crept stealthily on to the end of the bed and sat down on her feet. She fell asleep to the sound of his purr and taking great comfort from the warmth of his meagre small body through the blankets.

Life wasn't quite so dull any more; she had Buster to feed and talk to and he responded quickly enough to her gentle ways and quiet voice, taking a pride in his appearance once more, his small half-starved frame filling out nicely. As he kept out of Mrs Squires' way she forgot about him, since he prudently went in and out via the window and the roof. Deborah wrote to Trotty and told her about the cat and enlarged her days' activities so that they sounded quite interesting. Each time she wrote she longed to ask about Sir James but she didn't, hoping that Trotty would write about him—though she never did. Sir James enquired from time to time if she heard from Deborah and she told him what was in the letters without comment and each time he said, 'Oh, splendid,' without meaning it.

'He always was an obstinate little boy,' said Trotty to Maudie, 'and why he can't go to her and tell her he wants her for his wife I don't know.' Trotty blew her nose loudly as an alternative to having a good cry. 'I wish I had the dear child here, that I do.'

Deborah had lost her pink cheeks and the slight plumpness which Trotty's good food had given her. She was working hard and finding the shorthand difficult although she had mastered the typewriter well, but she had no speed yet and no means of practising between lessons. As for the word processor, her teacher, a forthright Cockney woman, made no bones about her doubts about Deborah making a success of it.

Deborah had stayed behind to ask some questions about her shorthand and the teacher stopped her as she was going out of the class room.

'You're a hard worker, I'll give you that,' she began 'but you're not the type; there's girls straight from school going into good jobs after several months here. Most of them understand computers too.'

Deborah put down her books and sat down at one of the desks. 'You mean I'll not get a job?'

'No, no, if you can speed up your typing and get the hang of the shorthand you ought to get work as a receptionist or a copy typist, but there's no future in that.

'I have to earn my living as soon as possible.'

'Yes, well, let's see how you're doing in a couple of weeks' time.'

A conversation which she repeated to Buster that night, lying in bed, unable to settle and sleep because the next door neighbours were holding a party with noisy abandon. Buster, who didn't care for loud voices or loud noises, had crept up close to her, draped over her shoulder and peering into her face, purring gently. She put out a hand and stroked his head; now that he had a life to his liking he had turned into a bit of a dandy, always beautifully groomed. He had even taught himself to purr in a soft rumble. He was a great comfort to her because she had no one else to talk to so she talked to him—about Maudie and Trotty and Bellum and Uncle Oscar and Mrs Vernon and inevitably Sir James. 'If I could just see him, Buster, then perhaps I would be able to forget him.'

She worked harder than ever, for the exams she was to take in two weeks' time were important, and if she failed them it would set her back weeks and there wouldn't be enough money to stay longer at the school. Her nest-egg was very nearly exhausted but once she had got her certificate she would take the first job she could find.

The exams were much worse than she had expected; she thought it unlikely that she had passed the shorthand test and she hadn't finished all the typing in time. The word processor she had been advised to drop since she was far too slow at it. All the same she went to bed that night feeling hopeful; a typing certificate would be better than nothing.

The results were on the noticeboard when she got to the school in the morning; she had failed both exams. Several others had failed too but they were young women who really had not cared if they passed or not. Now, they told her cheerfully, they would go on the dole. 'You can too,' they told her helpfully, 'you just sign on—if there's a job going you go and look at it and if you don't like it you say so.'

They all had families and homes to go to, and Social Security money was pocket money to them...

She thanked heaven that she had paid Mrs Squires her rent in advance; at least she had four or five days in which to look for work of some sort.

She went back to the shoddy little house and found it surprisingly silent. Mrs Squires seldom went out in the morning but there was no sign of her now. Deborah went to her room and found Buster fast asleep in his box. She supposed that there was no time like the present in which to start looking for a job, so she closed her door quietly and crossed the small landing to the stairs and then stopped to listen. Mrs Squires' door was closed but the sounds coming from behind it sounded very peculiar: great shuddering snorting sounds and then silences and then the snores again.

Deborah had never been in Mrs Squires' bedroom, indeed the only room she used in the house other than her own was the kitchen, and she hesitated for a moment before tapping on the door; Mrs Squires was a kind landlady but she had never encouraged anything more than a civil exchange of trivial remarks about mundane topics between the pair of them. All the same, the sounds didn't seem quite normal...

She tapped on the door again and no one answered although the snoring sounds continued. Hesitantly she went in. Mrs Squires was lying on the floor, alarmingly red in the face, her eyes half open and breathing in a stertorous manner.

There was no telephone in the house. Deborah ran to the corner shop and dialled for an ambulance, ran back to the house again, covered Mrs Squires with a blanket, put a pillow under her head and found the large nylon shopping bag her landlady used. Into it she stuffed whatever Mrs Squires was likely to need in hospital, then went back to her own room to make sure that Buster was still asleep, had food and could get out if he wanted to. It only remained for her to get her jacket, find her handbag and shut the windows and lock the back door then wait for the ambulance.

It came with commendable speed and the men were kind and gentle with Mrs Squires and wasted no time. There were no beds at the nearest hospital, they told Deborah, but the patient would have to be admitted and there was a bed in one of the big teaching hospitals and was she coming with them?

She watched them load the stretcher, locked the front door and got in with one of the men and Mrs Squires. Rattling through the streets, blue lights flashing, siren wailing, she reflected that, so far, it hadn't been her day. Nor, for that matter, she hastened to add guiltily, had it been for poor Mrs Squires.

It was quite a lengthy journey across the city and even with the siren going it was difficult to keep up any speed. 'Will she be all right?' asked Deborah, watching the paramedic using his skill on Mrs Squires.

He shrugged, 'Can't say, miss. It's a stroke and a massive one. We'll have to wait and see what they say.'

She followed the stretcher into casualty and went obediently to the reception desk to answer the receptionist's questions and then sit down in a corner near the curtained cubicle where Mrs Squires had been taken. There was a lot of coming and going, the place was crowded with patients and it was five minutes or more before a young doctor arrived, to be joined presently by an older man. Presently the nurse there hurried out, bent on some errand, and disappeared into the throng. Deborah looked at the clock, not really registering the time, wrapped in a bad dream and not capable of any sensible thought. She had done everything that was possible and now she wasn't sure what was expected of her. She had no idea if her landlady had any family; she had told the receptionist who had asked her to try and find out and let her know as soon as possible, but for the moment she thought she had better stay where she was.

The nurse came hurrying back and disappeared behind the curtains again and Deborah watched the people round her. It must be very interesting life, she thought, working in a hospital, but you needed to have A levels and to be able to pass exams. She looked away from the people waiting near her and watched one of the sisters coming towards her. Someone was there with her—Sir James.

He saw her as they drew level but he didn't pause in his stride, was ushered behind the curtains by the sister and it was a long time before he came out, this time with both the doctors and the sister hovering.

Deborah thought for one glorious moment that he was going to stop and speak to her, but even as he paused he was lifting the phone from the pocket of his long white coat and listening intently and, with a word to the older of the two doctors, going away. She would have felt better about it if she could have heard his abrupt, 'Who came with this lady?'

'No relation—the woman who lodges with her. Doesn't know much about her, unfortunately.'

Sir James was halfway to the lifts going fast. 'Get someone to ask her to wait. I'll see her presently.' He was borne aloft, his thoughts already concentrated upon his next patient.

There was a delay before Mrs Squires could be warded but Deborah didn't like to leave until she had been admitted to the women's medical where a busy ward sister spared a moment to explain that Mrs Squires was very ill and that Deborah should telephone later that evening. She frowned when Deborah explained that she wasn't a relation and indeed had no idea if there was one. 'I'll ask the neighbours and if I hear of one I'll telephone you, shall I?'

She went to look at Mrs Squires before she left the ward, lying so quietly in her bed, and, since the nurses were so busy, unpacked the things she had brought and put them in the locker by the bed.

It was on her way out that the receptionist called her over. 'There is a message for you from Sir James Marlow; you're to wait here, he wants to see you.'

Deborah thanked her politely and walked out of the door before anyone could stop her. It had been bad enough seeing him so unexpectedly and it had been even worse being looked at as though she wasn't there. She never wanted to see him again. By the time she had reached the bus stop she was in a towering rage, which was a good thing, for it prevented her from thinking of all the awful things which had happened that day.

CHAPTER NINE

IT was some time after Deborah had left Casualty before Sir James returned. The place was still busy but the receptionist had been on the lookout for him.

'I gave the young lady your message, sir,' she said, 'but she went away without a word.' She was dying of curiosity and would have put a leading question but the look on his face stopped her.

'He is always so polite and with beautiful manners as you know,' she said later, 'but he looked at me as though he could have wrung my neck. It wasn't my fault the girl went, was it?'

The receptionist taking over from her agreed and expressed the hope that he wouldn't come back while she was on duty, 'Mind you, I've always fancied him—that lovely car of his and he's rich—he must be...'

Sir James stifled an urge to leave the hospital at once and go after Deborah and went back to the women's medical and cast an eye over Mrs Squires, who despite his efforts was dying. All the same he intensified his fight for her life until there was no longer any need, then, leaving matters with his registrar, he got into his car and drove himself to the little terraced house near London Bridge.

The appearance of a gleaming Bentley caused something of a stir in the street but Deborah didn't hear it. The house had been cold and depressingly empty when she had got back, and since it was mid-afternoon by now she had put the kettle on, fed Buster and made herself a cup of tea before going to the corner shop to make enquiries about Mrs Squires' family. There was a brother, she was told, living on his own somewhere in Shoreditch, by the name of Whitmore, and if she knocked next door they might know his address.

It was surprising how helpful everyone was. Several neighbours volunteered information and the young man who lived in the end terrace house offered to get on to his motorbike and fetch Mr Whitmore; the rush-hour hadn't started and he'd have him at Mrs Squires' in no time at all.

Deborah thanked everyone and went back to the house and started to put Mrs Squires' bedroom to rights. She had no idea what would happen next but it seemed a good idea to make up the bed with clean linen and fill the washing machine. She Hoovered and dusted until a good deal of commotion in the street sent her to the door to find that the young man was back with Mr Whitmore hanging on rather frantically to the pillion. He was a small thin man with a sad moustache and watery eyes and he accepted her offer of the cup of tea with gratitude while she told him what had happened.

'I'd better go along to the hospital,' he said doubt-fully. 'There's no one else left but me. What's to happen to her?'

'I don't know,' said Deborah gently. 'She'll be kept there until she's much better and then perhaps she could go into a sheltered flat or something similar? This house is hers?'

'Yes, her hubby left it to her. I'm to have it when she goes.' He finished his tea while she explained that she was only lodging there and would be leaving at the end of the week. 'So the house will be empty, but I'll leave the keys and see it's clean and tidy.'

His face brightened at that. 'Well, I suppose there's not much to stop me moving in—kind of keep the place going until she comes home.' He got to his feet. 'I'll be off, then, and come in the morning so's we can sort things out a bit.'

After he had gone Deborah washed the cups once more and tackled the kitchen. Mrs Squires hadn't been a good housewife, or perhaps she had just lost interest living on her own—the kitchen needed to be thoroughly turned out and she was glad to have worthwhile things to do. However hard she worked, she couldn't stop her thoughts. A brisk tattoo on the doorknocker brought her head out of the kitchen cupboard; a neighbour probably with an offer of supper; she had been rather touched by all the help offered to her.

She didn't bother to take off the apron of Mrs Squires's that she had on; everyone knew she was seeing to the housework and besides almost all the women in the street wore an apron for a good deal of their day.

She opened the door and Sir James walked in and to her utter dismay she burst into tears at the sight of him and his vast reassuring person and flung herself on to his waistcoat.

He said nothing, but let her cry, and presently when her snivelling gave way to heaving sobs he took one arm from her and offered her a beautifully laundered handkerchief.

She wriggled free then, mopped her face and blew her nose resolutely.

'I'm so sorry.' Her voice was still thick with tears. 'But it's been a simply beastly day.'

He stood in the little hall, watching her and said presently, 'Why did you not wait, Deborah?'

She glared at him and gave a defiant sniff. 'You looked at me as though—as though...' Words failed her and she tried again. 'Whenever we meet I'm in trouble and it's always you there and you must be so tired of helping me...' She drew a breath, aware that she hadn't explained very well. 'I've tried, I really have, to keep out of your way.' She suddenly remembered that the day had begun badly and didn't say any more in case she started to cry again.

Sir James, it seemed, had nothing to say; presently she asked, 'Is Mrs Squires going to be all right?'

'She died shortly after she was warded. There was almost nothing to be done, I'm afraid.'

Deborah said in a small voice, 'She was very kind, you know. Trotty will be sad...'

'What else has gone wrong with your day?' asked Sir James in a voice to charm the birds off the trees.

She hadn't meant to tell him, but it came tumbling out. 'I failed my exams—I was taking shorthand and typing, you know, and I thought if I passed the exams at the end of the course I could get a job and move somewhere else and start a career.'

Anyone looking less like a career girl would be hard to find, thought Sir James with tender amusement: hair on end, a grubby apron, a small red nose and puffy eyes from crying. He said in a kind voice, 'Well, you can consider that in the morning. You will come home with me now, Deborah.'

'Home with you? Indeed I won't. I'm cleaning the house and besides, I can't leave Buster.' He raised his eyebrows and she explained about Buster. 'The very idea . . .' she finished, reminding herself that the quicker he went away, really away and out of her life, the better.

Sir James utilised his impressive bedside manner, kind and considerate but beneath his calm a rock-hard determination to get his own way. 'You will do as I say, Deborah. Go upstairs and pack a bag for the night and find the cat. I will bring you back in the morning but you are not to sleep here alone tonight.'

She opened her mouth ready to utter a defiant, 'I won't,' but caught his eye and thought better of it. She backed towards the stairs. 'Well, all right, but Mr Whitmore is coming in the morning—Mrs Squires' brother, he's gone to the hospital . . .'

'You will be here when he arrives so that you can make whatever arrangements are necessary.'

She packed a small case and bore the sleeping Buster downstairs in his box. Sir James was standing where she had left him but the door and windows were shut, all but the hall light out and the bucket of dirty water by the cupboard emptied and set tidily in the sink.

He took her case from her, peered at Buster and opened the car door so that she might put his box on the back seat. Then he shut the door, ushered her into the front of the car, told her to stay there and knocked on the door of the next house. There were faces peering from several windows and the neighbour came

to the door with alacrity and stood listening while Sir
James talked. Deborah had no idea what he was saying
but the neighbour nodded a great deal and smiled and
then waved to her before Sir James turned away and
got into the car.

He leaned over and fastened her seatbelt. 'Had your
tea?' he asked, and when she shook her head,
'Lunch?' and she muttered something and he said,
'I'm sure Mrs Dobbs, my housekeeper, will have
something nice for us.'

He smiled at her so kindly that she had to clench
her teeth to keep from crying again, indeed, once he
had started the car and perforce couldn't look at her,
she allowed the tears to trickle soundlessly down her
cheeks. It was dark anyway even though the streets
were brightly lighted and she turned her head and
looked out of the window, not caring where they were
going.

Since it was on the other side of the city it took
twenty minutes or so and by then she was feeling much
more herself. Still looking out of the window, she blew
her nose, wiped her eyes and turned to look ahead of
her.

'Feeling better?' asked Sir James cheerfully.
'There's nothing like a good cry.' He didn't look at
her. 'We're almost there.'

They were in more spacious streets now and presently when he drove down a narrow side-street and
stopped before his elegant house she said in an effort
to be polite, 'It's very nice here...'

He agreed blandly, offering the information that it
was handy for his work. He got out and opened her
door and reached inside for Buster in his box. Buster

was annoyed and a little frightened; Deborah had tied
a teatowel over his box to keep him safe and he did
not like it. She took the box from Sir James and followed him across the pavement and up the few steps
to his front door, opened as they reached it by Dobbs
who wished his master a gloomy 'Good evening', and,
being introduced to Deborah, inclined his head with
civil gravity, taking in every detail of her appearance
as he did so.

'Ask Mrs Dobbs to come here, will you, Dobbs?
Miss Everett would like to tidy herself. She will be
staying the night so get someone to see that there's a
room ready, will you?' His glance fell on the box in
her arms; the tea cloth was heaving dangerously. 'We
have got a cat with us—Deborah, what do you think
would be the best thing to do with Buster?'

'If you wouldn't mind having him for just a few
minutes while I do my hair...he could stay in his
box...he's used to me and I think he'll stay quiet
once I sit down.' She added, 'But where's Bellum?'

'Asleep?' Sir James looked at Dobbs.

'In the garden, sir.'

'Right—let him in, will you?' He cast an eye over
Deborah. 'Run along—I'll look after Buster.'

Doing the best she could with her tearstained face
and untidy head, Deborah had to admit that it was
comforting to have someone telling her what to do,
arranging this for her. She powdered her nose lavishly
and redid her hair and wished with all her heart that
she were beautiful and that soon Sir James would take
one look at her and fall deeply in love.

Which, if she did but know it, was exactly what he
did do as she came back into the hall; at least he had

always thought her beautiful and he fell rather more deeply in love at the sight of her, hesitating by the cloakroom door.

'Over here.' He opened the door wide and she went past him into his sitting-room. It was a delightful place, cosily furnished with comfortable chairs and a huge sofa before the fire and behind it a lovely Pembroke table. There were lamps on the small tables and a Georgian breakfront bookcase in mahogany against one wall. Buster was sitting on top of it and Bellum was sitting in front of the fire, wagging his tail.

'Oh—is he safe?'

'I told Bellum to sit—he's an obedient dog, besides he is used to Mrs Dobbs' cat and Trotty's Maudie. Come and sit down. Will you have a drink? A glass of sherry?'

He put the glass on a small tripod table by her chair and went to sit down opposite her, a glass of whisky at his elbow.

'How long have you been with Mrs Squires? A friend of Trotty's, you said?'

Deborah, unaware that he was perfectly aware of how long she had been there—had in fact, received news of her from Trotty—explained. She didn't do it very well; the sherry was going to her head, she was tired and sad, and mixed in with all these feelings was the predominant one of her love for James sitting there, only yards away, so near and yet so very far... She came to a stumbling halt and he observed mildly that for the moment her circumstances were unfortunate, but that something was bound to turn up.

She was saved from answering this by Dobbs, coming to tell them that Mrs Dobbs had dinner ready if Sir James was agreeable.

At the door Deborah turned to look at Buster. 'You don't mind my leaving him there? Bellum won't hurt him and he might break something...'

'We will leave them to get used to the sight of each other,' said Sir James and ushered her across the hall into the dining-room.

Dobbs had always prided himself on his elegant table arrangements even when his master was alone; now he had laid a lace-edged cloth with silver and crystal and the Worcester china he cherished for a dinner party and he had placed a bowl of pink roses and mint leaves at the centre. He looked as gloomy as ever but in the kitchen he had informed his wife that he could smell romance in the air, and was gratified to hear her agree. 'A nice young lady, very quiet, I thought, and lovely eyes.'

Deborah realised as they sat down that she was famished; breakfast had been early and sketchy because she had wanted to get to the school in good time for the results, lunch had been forgotten entirely although she had made a cup of tea... Mrs Dobbs' asparagus soup, made as it should be from fresh asparagus and not out of a tin, and with a little thin cream stirred in at the last moment, was the best thing she had tasted for a long time, or so she thought until the duckling with an orange and honey sauce came, and that was followed by a fruit tart so light that the pastry melted in one's mouth. She drank the wine she was offered, prudently refusing a second glass before they went back to the sitting-room, where Dobbs had put the coffee tray. Halfway to the hearth she stopped. 'Buster—he's gone?'

Sir James put a reassuring hand on her arm. 'Look,' he advised her.

Buster and Bellum were sitting side by side, not looking at each other, staring into the fire, but presently when Deborah was sitting in a chair again Buster crept up on to her lap where he stayed until, after an hour's desultory talk which never once touched on Deborah's situation, Sir James suggested that she might like an early night. 'You must be tired and I'm afraid that we must leave quite early tomorrow morning—I have a clinic at half-past eight and I want to drive you back to Mrs Squires' house first.'

'I'll catch a bus...'

His eye fell on Buster, sitting so quietly on her lap in a guarded way. Sir James said mildly, 'I don't think Buster would like that. We will leave at half-past seven—breakfast at seven; someone will call you in good time.'

She was tired and so dispirited with impossible ideas as to where she would go or what she would do flitting through her head that she said meekly, 'Very well, Sir James,' and then, 'What shall I do with Buster?'

'He may accompany you if you wish. Your room has an enclosed balcony and Dobbs will have arranged things.'

She got to her feet with Buster under one arm. 'You think of everything. Thank you very much for my dinner—and letting me sleep here.'

He had got up too and went to open the door for her. 'Sleep well, Deborah,' was all he said.

She slept like the proverbial log and so did Buster, who ate his breakfast on the balcony while she went downstairs to eat hers with Sir James. They had it in a small, very cosy room behind the dining-room and since there wasn't much time their conversation was no more than requests to pass the toast or the coffee-pot. He had said half-past seven and they left exactly then, driving through the still fairly empty streets. There was no hanging about once they reached Mrs Squires' house. He took the house key from her, opened the door, took a quick look round and carried her case indoors.

'Thank you very much,' said Deborah, 'and do go quickly or you'll be late. Drive carefully, won't you?' She put a hand on his. 'Goodbye.'

He took her hand and didn't let it go. 'You will pack your things—all of them. I will be here soon after six o'clock.'

She tugged at her hand, and felt his clasp tighten. 'Why?'

'What a girl you are for asking questions when I have no time to answer them. I am driving you down to Trotty, of course. You'll stay there until we have considered your future.' When she opened her mouth to protest, he said, 'No, don't argue, I haven't the time.' He smiled suddenly. 'Be a dear girl and do just as I ask.'

'Buster...?'

'Naturally Buster will accompany you.' He got into the car and drove off with a casual wave. No one had ever told him to drive carefully before; it had sounded very wifelike and she had looked endearingly anxious. He was going to be late at his consulting-rooms but

Alice would see that his first patient was well taken care of. As soon as he started to drive he began to map out his day. It was going to be a busy one—it would be late by the time he got back from Trotty's cottage that night and the following morning he was going to be even busier. He got out of his car in Harley Street and went up the stairs to his consulting-rooms, the mantle of his profession already on his broad shoulders.

It was still early morning when Deborah closed the door of Mrs Squires' house, donned the apron once more, released Buster from his box and boiled a kettle of water. There was a good deal of cleaning to do and Mr Whitmore would probably want coffee when he came. She filled her bucket and finished cleaning out the kitchen cupboard before giving the sink a good scrub. There was the bedlinen from her bed to wash too; she hung the first lot on the line in the narrow back garden and stripped her bed, set the machine going and turned her attention to the sitting-room. The house and its furniture began to gleam with soap and polish. By the time Mr Whitmore arrived, another lot of washing was out to dry and she had put coffee and sugar on the clean kitchen table with two mugs. All this time she had been constantly interrupted by the neighbours, calling to see if they could help and glean any news.

Mr Whitmore had smartened himself up, explaining his best suit by telling her that he had been to see his sister's solicitor. 'To get things sorted out,' he explained. And it was quite all right for him to move in whenever he liked; the house was his now.

He looked round with a proprietorial air and then at Deborah.

'I've cleaned the house and left everything just so,' she told him. 'I'm being fetched by a friend this evening. You won't mind if I stay here until about six o'clock?'

He looked relieved; possibly, she reflected, he had expected her to ask to stay until she could find somewhere else to go. 'Suits me,' he told her. 'I've got my things to pack up. If I'm not back by the time you go, can you leave the key with someone?'

'The neighbour will take it, I'm sure. Would you like to go round the house before you go?'

He agreed to that, looking askance at Buster, perched on top of the wardrobe in her room. 'It's all right,' said Deborah. 'Buster is going with me. Mrs Squires gave him to me.'

'Don't hold with cats,' muttered Mr Whitmore, and presently he went away.

She packed her things then, folded the clean washing, watered the plants and fed Buster before using up the last of the bread and a tin of beans for her lunch.

She hung the pinny behind the door, washed her face and hands and did her hair in its coil before wasting a lot of time on her face. She needed creams and lotions and the exact shade of powder and several lipsticks before she could look even faintly pretty; she peered at her reflection and decided that there was nothing more to be done. She might as well have some tea ...

She was going round the house, bolting and locking doors and windows, when the Bentley came to a slow

silent halt before the door. She stood at the bedroom
window and watched Sir James get out without haste
and thump the knocker. He was so quiet and so sure
of himself and so kind . . . She stifled a sigh and went
down to let him in.

'You're ready? Wait a moment while I get a basket
for Buster, he'll be more comfortable than in that box.'

He came back with a cat basket, a roomy one with
one end covered in a fine mesh so that the occupant
could look out if he wished to. Buster, protesting hotly,
was transferred and put on the back seat while she
took the key next door and made her goodbyes. Sir
James put the two cases in the boot and opened her
door, all with a kindly impersonal air which she found
daunting.

Perhaps he had had second thoughts, she mused
worriedly, or he had had to break some engagement
for the evening in order to drive her to Trotty.

They drove in silence for a few minutes before she
ventured, 'I hope I haven't upset your plans . . .'

'No, no, in fact you have fallen in with them very
nicely.'

She thought this over for a minute or two and could
make nothing of it at first, then she concluded that
he had intended to visit Trotty anyway.

The rush-hour was easing a little but it was still a
slow business crossing the city. She sat quietly, not
wishing to distract his attention from the traffic
around him. At some traffic lights he glanced at her.

'I'm driving carefully enough for you, Deborah?'

'Oh, did you think that I thought you were a bad
driver? It wasn't that at all—I wouldn't like you to
get hurt . . .'

The lights changed and he drove on, his face impassive; only his eyes gleamed under their lids. Just for a moment he was tempted to call his registrar and tell him that he wouldn't be at the hospital in the morning; but he had waited so long, he reflected, that he could—must—wait for one more day. Alice could cancel his private patients and book them in for the following day and he would have to warn Dobbs. Behind a placid face he rearranged his day so that he would be free to drive down to Trotty's and talk to Deborah.

'Where's Bellum?' asked Deborah suddenly.

'At home. I thought it might be rather more than Buster could stand, imprisoned in a basket with a dog breathing all over him.'

'Oh, poor Bellum, did he hate being left behind?'

'Very much—but he knows I'll be back this evening.'

Beyond asking her if she was comfortable he had little to say and after one or two tentative remarks she fell silent, supposing that he was thinking about his patients. Once clear of London and the suburbs, travelling at the maximum speed along the motorway, the journey seemed short, too short for Deborah, watching his large well-kept hands on the wheel, wanting to look at his face but staring ahead of her instead. He hadn't told her how long she was to stay at Trotty's cottage; she supposed for as long as it took her to get another job, something she would deal with with the utmost urgency. Really, she reflected, life for the last few months had been a series of jobs which somehow came to an end only to find him waiting for her, so to speak. Just his bad luck, she told herself briskly, and remarked brightly that they were almost there.

Trotty welcomed them warmly, accepted Buster in his basket and by now in a bad temper with a calm briskness, and when Sir James, having unloaded the cases and carried them upstairs, told her that he was going straight back to town, said roundly that he was to sit down at the kitchen table immediately and drink a cup of coffee. Deborah was told to sit down too as soon as she had released Buster into the scullery with all the doors shut and a bowl of food for him to gobble.

'Peaky, that's just what you look, Deborah,' declared Trotty. 'Fresh air and some good food, that's what you need. You shall tell me about Mrs Squires presently. I must say that was a bit of a shock.'

She stood over them while they drank their coffee and went to the door with Sir James. He got up unhurriedly, bade Deborah to stay where she was and do as Trotty told her, and went out to his car, and Trotty went with him. She came back presently, looking smug, but Deborah was thinking about Sir James and didn't notice. He hadn't even said goodbye; he certainly hadn't listened to her polite speech of thanks. He had this awful habit of going away suddenly, leaving her feeling as though she had lost an arm or a leg.

She looked at Trotty with an unhappy face. 'I'm no good at anything, Trotty, and he always turns up when things have gone wrong and I'm being such an awful nuisance. I'm not being sorry for myself but I don't seem to be able to get away from him.' She took a deep breath. 'But I will, I'll get another job as quickly as I can and save some money and take a typing course again.'

'Splendid,' said Trotty bracingly, 'but first a couple of days here; it's no good dashing off to the first job that's offered. Besides, you could do with a bit of feeding up. And that cat of yours, a few breaths of country air will do him good too.'

'What about Maudie?'

'Bless you, child, she'll soon have him in his place. The kittens are all away to good homes and it'll give her an interest in life, getting him to toe the line.' Trotty took the mugs to the sink. 'Up you go and wash your face and unpack and we'll have supper and then bed for you.'

Trotty's kindly tyranny was soothing and comforting. Deborah did as she was told and presently, nicely full of supper and warm from a hot bath, she got into bed. Her bedroom door left open so that Buster, should he wish, could go downstairs to the scullery.

Trotty was a splendid listener. For most of the next day Deborah talked. There was such a lot to tell; Mrs Squires and the school and her work, failing her exams, the kindness of the neighbours and, although she tried not to talk too much about Sir James, of course she did.

Trotty plied her with good food, good advice with common sense and matter-of-fact suggestions for the future. Another day or two, she was told, and then she could go to Reading or Henley and find a good agency. At the end of the second day Deborah asked with careful casualness if Sir James would be coming again.

'Now, would I ask him something like that?' Trotty wanted to know. 'And him so busy examining all those poor souls with their addled brains, getting them better too I have no doubt.' She spoke rather tartly; she wouldn't tell a lie unless she really had to and she was pleased with the way she had got out of that one and had answered Deborah without erring from the truth. 'What about going to Henley tomorrow? It's a bit of a journey but you might find it worth your while.'

Deborah agreed in a bright voice and presently took herself off to bed.

She woke early and since there was no point in lying in bed dreaming about Sir James, she got into her dressing-gown, a dreary, colourless garment entirely lacking glamour, stuck her feet into her equally dull slippers and padded downstairs. She would make a cup of tea and take one to Trotty...

Sir James was sitting at the kitchen table, Bellum at his feet, a pot of tea on the table before him, a mug in his hand. He looked up as she went in and got to his feet. His, 'Good morning, Deborah,' was uttered in a placid voice.

'James,' said Deborah, quite forgetting herself. 'Oh, James, you've come.'

She regretted the words the minute she had said them but they were out now and she would have to make the best of it. 'What I mean is,' she said carefully, 'that it's nice to see you...'

'Oh, good. Have a mug of tea. I've taken one up to Trotty.'

'You haven't been here all night?'

'No, no, I got here about an hour ago.' He pulled a chair from the table. 'Sit down do—there, with the table between us. Bellum, sit.'

Bellum, overjoyed at the sight of Deborah, sat, and Sir James poured the tea, offered her milk and sugar and then resumed his seat, his conversation apparently exhausted.

For something to say Deborah embarked on the rather disjointed information that she was going into Henley to find a job.

Sir James put down his mug. 'No, you're not.' He smiled at her. 'You're coming to the cottage with me.'

She put her mug down too because her hands were shaking so. 'You have been very kind, Sir James, but I am going to Henley...'

'I suppose it's your hair which makes you so pigheaded. I am taking you to the cottage. Do you want to know why?'

She tossed a fiery tress of hair over her shoulder and looked him in the eye. 'Yes.'

'I am going to ask you to marry me, Deborah, and for some reason I want to do it in my own home, preferably in the garden with no one looking on.'

He leaned forward and took the mug from her and took her hand and kissed her palm. 'I have given you every opportunity of leading your own life but now my patience is quite exhausted. In any case I can see that the only career in which you will be successful is as my wife, making sure that I drive carefully and am never late for work and welcoming me back home each evening, preferably with a clutch of children.'

'But I'm not suitable...'

'My dearest love, what is all this nonsense about being suitable? I'm in love with you—have been for a long time now—and I love you...'

'Oh, is there a difference?'

'Indeed there is.'

'Well, if you don't mind my not being suitable, I would very much like to marry you. I love you too.'

Sir James got up and went round the table and pulled her gently to her feet. He held her so close that her ribs ached. 'This is by way of being a dress rehearsal,' he told her, 'but it will do for a start.' He began to kiss her then, very thoroughly and at some length. 'My darling girl, will you mind if we marry very soon, just as soon as I can get a licence? I shall have to go back to London this evening but you will stay at the cottage until I come again...' He kissed her once more. 'Now go and put on some clothes and throw away that blanket thing you're wearing.'

She reached up to put her arms around his neck. 'I can't do that. I haven't another one.'

'Easily remedied. We'll buy one for every day of the week.'

She kissed him and Trotty came into the kitchen, as neat as a new pin. 'Bacon and eggs for breakfast,' she said briskly. 'Put some clothes on, love.'

Sir James still held Deborah close. 'We're going to be married, Trotty.'

'And high time too,' said Trotty, as she reached for the frying-pan. 'I shall buy a new hat...'

'As many hats as you like, Trotty,' said Sir James. He smiled down at Deborah, kissed the top of her head very gently and gave her a little push towards the door. 'My beautiful girl,' he said very softly into her ear.

Deborah smiled. It was an extraordinary thing, but she actually felt beautiful.

BRIDE'S BAY RESORT

UNLOCK THE DOOR TO GREAT ROMANCE AT BRIDE'S BAY RESORT

Join Harlequin's new across-the-lines series, set in an exclusive hotel on an island off the coast of South Carolina.

Seven of your favorite authors will bring you exciting stories about fascinating heroes and heroines discovering love at Bride's Bay Resort.

Look for these fabulous stories coming to a store near you beginning in January 1996.

Harlequin American Romance #613 in January
Matchmaking Baby by Cathy Gillen Thacker

Harlequin Presents #1794 in February
Indiscretions by Robyn Donald

Harlequin Intrigue #362 in March
Love and Lies by Dawn Stewardson

Harlequin Romance #3404 in April
Make Believe Engagement by Day Leclaire

Harlequin Temptation #588 in May
Stranger in the Night by Roseanne Williams

Harlequin Superromance #695 in June
Married to a Stranger by Connie Bennett

Harlequin Historicals #324 in July
Dulcie's Gift by Ruth Langan

Visit Bride's Bay Resort each month wherever Harlequin books are sold.

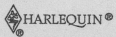

HARLEQUIN®

BBAYG

MILLION DOLLAR SWEEPSTAKES
AND
EXTRA BONUS PRIZE DRAWING

No purchase necessary. To enter the sweepstakes, follow the directions published and complete and mail your Official Entry Form. If your Official Entry Form is missing, or you wish to obtain an additional one (limit: one Official Entry Form per request, one request per outer mailing envelope) send a separate, stamped, self-addressed #10 envelope (4 1/8" X 9 1/2") via first-class mail to: Million Dollar Sweepstakes and Extra Bonus Prize Drawing Entry Form, P.O. Box 1867, Buffalo, NY 14269-1867. Request must be received no later than January 15, 1998. For eligibility into the sweepstakes, entries must be received no later than March 31,1998. No liability is assumed for printing errors, lost, late, non-delivered or misdirected entries. Odds of winning are determined by the number of eligible entries distributed and received.

Sweepstakes open to residents of the U.S. (except Puerto Rico), Canada and Europe who are 18 years of age or older. All applicable laws and regulations apply. Sweepstakes offer void wherever prohibited by law. Values of all prizes are in U.S. currency. This sweepstakes is presented by Torstar Corp., its subsidiaries and affiliates, in conjuction with book, merchandise and/or product offerings. For a copy of the Official Rules governing this sweepstakes, send a self-addressed, stamped envelope (WA residents need not affix return postage) to: MILLION DOLLAR SWEEP-STAKES AND EXTRA BONUS PRIZE DRAWING Rules, P.O. Box 4470, Blair, NE 68009-4470, USA.

FAST CASH 4033 DRAW RULES
NO PURCHASE OR OBLIGATION NECESSARY

Fifty prizes of $50 each will be awarded in random drawings to be conducted no later than 6/28/96 from amongst all eligible responses to this prize offer received as of 5/14/96. To enter, follow directions, affix 1st-class postage and mail OR write Fast Cash 4033 on a 3" x 5" card along with your name and address and mail that card to: Harlequin's Fast Cash 4033 Draw, P.O. Box 1395, Buffalo, NY 14240-1395 OR P.O. Box 618, Fort Erie, Ontario L2A 5X3. (Limit: one entry per outer envelope; all entries must be sent via 1st-class mail.) Limit: one prize per household. Odds of winning are determined by the number of eligible responses received. Offer is open only to resi-dents of the U.S. (except Puerto Rico) and Canada and is void wherever prohibited by law. All applicable laws and regulations apply. Any litigation within the province of Quebec respecting the conduct and awarding of a prize in this sweepstakes may be submitted to the Régie des alcools, des courses et des jeux. In order for a Canadian resident to win a prize, that person will be required to correctly answer a time-limited arithmetical skill-testing question to be administered by mail. Names of winners available after 7/30/96 by sending a self-addressed, stamped envelope to: Fast Cash 4033 Draw Winners, P.O. Box 4200, Blair, NE 68009-4200.

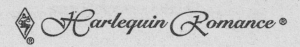

New from Harlequin Romance
a very special six-book series by

The town of Hard Luck, Alaska, needs women!

The O'Halloran brothers, who run a bush-plane service called **Midnight Sons**, are heading a campaign to attract women to Hard Luck. *(Location: north of the Arctic Circle. Population: 150—mostly men!)*

"Debbie Macomber's *Midnight Sons* series is a delightful romantic saga. And each book is a powerful, engaging story in its own right. Unforgettable!"

—Linda Lael Miller

TITLE IN THE MIDNIGHT SONS SERIES:

DMS-1

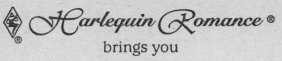
Harlequin Romance ®

brings you

How the West Was Wooed!

We've rounded up twelve of our most popular authors,
and the result is a whole year of romance, Western
style. Every month we'll be bringing you a spirited,
independent woman whose heart is about to be lassoed
by a rugged, handsome, one-hundred-percent cowboy!
Watch for...

- April: A DANGEROUS MAGIC—Patricia Wilson

- May: THE BADLANDS BRIDE—Rebecca Winters

- June: RUNAWAY WEDDING—Ruth Jean Dale

- July: A RANCH, A RING AND EVERYTHING—Val Daniels

- August: TEMPORARY TEXAN—Heather Allison

HITCH-3

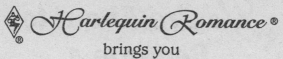

Harlequin Romance ®

brings you

HOLDING
HER☆
OUT FOR A

Some men are worth waiting for!

They're handsome, they're charming but, best of all, they're single! Twelve lucky women are about to discover that finding Mr. Right is not a problem—it's holding on to him.

In April the series continues with

#3406 THE RIGHT KIND OF MAN
by Jessica Hart

Skye had run away from man trouble, only to bump smack into Lorimer Kingan. He was tall, dark and handsome, and he wanted an efficient, reliable PA. Skye desperately wanted the job, but could she really describe herself as *efficient?* Worse, she knew as soon as she saw him that Lorimer was the right kind of man for her!

Hold out for Harlequin Romance's heroes in coming months...

- May: **MOVING IN WITH ADAM**—Jeanne Allan

- June: **THE DADDY TRAP**—Leigh Michaels

- July: **THE BACHELOR'S WEDDING**—Betty Neels

HOFH-4

You're About to Become a *Privileged Woman*

Reap the rewards of fabulous free gifts and benefits with proofs-of-purchase from Harlequin and Silhouette books

Pages & Privileges™

It's our way of thanking you for buying our books at your favorite retail stores.

PROOF OF PURCHASE
Offer expires October 31, 1996
HR-PP118

Harlequin and Silhouette— the most privileged readers in the world!

For more information about Harlequin and Silhouette's PAGES & PRIVILEGES program call the Pages & Privileges Benefits Desk: 1-503-794-2499

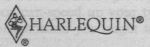

HARLEQUIN®

HR-PP118